The Shoemaker's Dream
a Jewish American immigrant story

Warm best wishes —
Bill Nemoyten
Hayward, CA
5/1/2018

The Shoemaker's Dream

a Jewish American
immigrant story

by Bill Nemoyten

Edited by Teja Watson

Introduction by Marilyn J. Boxer

a foolish tree book
san francisco
2018

The Shoemaker's Dream
a Jewish American immigrant story

Published by foolish tree, 280 Granada Avenue #2, San Francisco, CA 94112.
info@foolishtreebooks.com
foolishtreebooks.com/shoemaker

This story is based on the historical facts available as well as the memories of
the author and his relatives. From there, the author has embellished the tale,
hoping to evoke an experience of what life was like for his mother's family.
Most of the characters are real people while some are entirely fictional.

Cover and interior design by Jo Nemoyten.
Cover and interior images from free Creative Commons sources and by
various family members and friends of the author.

ISBN-13: 978-0692090480 (foolish tree)
ISBN-10: 0692090487

This book is dedicated to the memory of Dr. Phillip Lerner.

Cousins "Billy" and Phillip
Ages 10 and 6
Cleveland

Table of Contents

Foreword

The Shoemaker's Dream was the "American Dream" shared by millions of people speaking countless languages in countries around the world, and it brought to our shores the people who fashioned this vast and powerful nation. This iconic metaphor has served for generations to express the dreamers' hopes of achieving a better future for themselves and their families. This is a tale that resonates strongly today, when news media daily produce articles, editorials and letters to the editor about our current political embattlement over immigration. Like so many today, the shoemaker's relation whose adventures are told in these pages landed in America in 1910 speaking no English, with minimal financial resources, but endowed with boundless ambition, hope, energy, and desire. While building new lives, they built our country.

As Bill Nemoyten opens his multigenerational saga, he tells the story of his great-uncle-in-law, Avrum Binstock, a shoemaker in a village in Poland who aspired to expand his artisanal shop into a factory, readers learn of life in the "Old Country." He carries us across the sea with his uncle, the shoemaker's nephew, Israel Zynger, later Izzy Singer. Unlike many tales of immigrants to the United States—or, more poetically named, America—which begin with their arrival on the shores of the "New World," Nemoyten takes us back to their origins. As friends and colleagues in Kol Hadash, the Northern Californian Community for Humanistic Judaism, Bill and I have heard in our annual "modern exodus" Seders of many Jewish families who experienced narrow and harrowing escapes from persecution and poverty. But there, too, we learn little of the life they left behind. It was, in the minds of many of our forebears, best forgotten. Today, we want to know more.

Here, in this novelized version of Bill's family history, we go beyond numbers about immigration and assimilation to relive life on the other side of the ocean. We learn about the life they left behind: the terror of pogroms led by tsarist soldiers or gentile neighbors, signaled by shouts and crying in the streets; the dreaded knock on the door when sons reached the age of conscription into army service for perhaps twenty years, from which all-too-many never returned; but also the pleasures of market days when these gatherings provided the main venue for buying, selling, and exchanging news of local events, long before "farmers' markets" became a fashionable alternative to shopping at giant, industrialized emporia. Bill helps us as well to feel the love and respect accorded in Jewish communities to the scribe and scholar who made the words of ancient scripture accessible to their less educated coreligionists.

We learn, too, of the warmth shared among extended families, often, as resources allowed, brought serially to America. Continued for a while, like the I. Singer Unity Club named for Izzy, it offered a kind of solidarity rarely seen among later generations of Jews, who had fewer children and saw many of them scatter across the vast reaches of this new land, to follow opportunities never open to them before. Despite this, however, they maintained many traditions, for instance bringing to the United States the "Family Free Loan Society" used by Jewish families in Eastern Europe to support each other in times of need with interest-free loans, imported to the United States as a Hebrew Free Loan association, and now established in cities across the country as well as in Argentina, Australia, and Israel (and not limited to Jewish individuals).

All this provides the context for Bill's narrative, one family's history that illuminates migration history writ small. He follows the ambitious adventures of Izzy Singer, formerly Israel Zynger, as he departs from Losice, Poland, and travels via Warsaw, Antwerp, London, Ellis Island, and New York City to Cleveland, where Bill would be born in 1928. Despite occasional misadventures, once he passed the physical exam at Ellis Island, Izzy could proceed according to his own lights, never threatened as are many today with the question, "Do you have papers?" None were needed. He was welcome to test his mettle, free to transfer his leather-cutting skills from Poland to fur-making in Ohio.

Vividly recounted, brought to life with imagined dialogue, and embellished with the zest accumulated through his own adventurous life (as told by Bill in his 2012 book, *It All Started with a Trombone: The Hornman Memoirs*), Izzy's story includes drama, such as Dina's daring effort to rescue her already-conscripted son from the clutches of the czarist army; romance, in the four-year-long correspondence of Izzy with Dorothy, as she grows to marriageable age; suspense, when a shop fire erupts on the eve of Izzy's and Dorothy's wedding; and even a little sex, when Rosh Hashana fell on Shabbat. It acquaints us with a diverse set of characters, from Boris, the businessman who, along with a meal of gefilte fish and a spot of Slivovitz, gives Avrum an introduction to the new thought of the *Haskalah* (Enlightenment); and Koppy, the man-of-many-talents but no regular job who teaches the "greenhorn" Izzy the street smarts he needs to survive amid the toughs of Manhattan. The benevolent furrier Solomon appreciates Izzy's diligence and entrepreneurial spirit, and rewards him bountifully. With an epilogue that summarizes the many individual successes and collective contributions to American (and Israeli) society of several generations of descendants of the shoemaker, Avrum Binstock, and his nephew, Israel Zynger, Bill concludes his tale of Jewish immigrants who built new lives here and helped to build America and its institutions.

Marilyn J. Boxer
Professor of History Emerita
San Francisco State University

Introduction

Following World War I, hundreds of thousands of Jewish refugees from Eastern Europe fled their native lands of Russia, Poland, Romania, Hungary, Lithuania, and many other countries, in an effort to seek freedom from oppression in its many forms: despotic rulers, forced military conscription, lack of freedom, lack of opportunities to better their lives. Many emigrated to England, France, and other Western European nations, and some to Palestine. But the place most of them wanted to come to was the United States, where they heard the opportunities were the greatest. Some had even believed the rumor that in America the streets were paved with gold.

The journey by sea to that faraway land was costly and hazardous. And yet, so many parents were willing to make the sacrifices necessary to make it possible for their children and grandchildren to live more fulfilled lives. There was a pattern of how this was accomplished that held true in many families. Often, the oldest son was sent to America. He was expected to find work and save his money, in order to be able to bring the rest of his family to New York, or New Jersey, or Boston, or any one of hundreds of big cities and small towns across America.

Part One of this book is derived from information shared with me by Fred Binstock, grandson of the principal character of that part of the story, Avrum Binstock. Fred's research revealed that Avrum was a shoemaker in Losice, Poland. He created a shoemaking factory in his home and regularly traveled to Warsaw to sell his shoes and boots. He would then buy more materials, in order to continue the process of manufacturing and return to Warsaw to sell them.

The fact that his grandfather was a shoemaker was not surprising. I knew Fred's father, a cousin of my mother's, who came to Cleveland right after World War II, somehow surviving the infamous Auschwitz death camp. Herschel was a skilled shoe and boot-maker. Perhaps his services were valued by his Nazi captors; that could be why he escaped extermination. After the war, he met and married Leah Konigsberg, also a Holocaust survivor. Herschel died several years ago. Leah, mother of two sons and a daughter, lives in Cleveland and is a remarkable, tiny woman who has survived into her nineties. Except for the few facts derived from what Fred Binstock related to me, all the rest of Part One is a fictional story.

Parts Two and Three of this book are fictional stories based on a booklet written by my cousin, Dr. Phillip Lerner. He entitled it "Cousins: The Next Generation." His information was gathered from his mother, my Aunt Pearl Lerner, and from several of my first cousins, who are all the grandchildren of Chaim Singer. I have taken the factual material—which tells what happened, but not how it happened—and have filled in the details about how life might have been lived by my grandparents, my mother, and my aunts and uncles in the early part of the twentieth century. Using my imagination, I created a story that I hope will be exciting and pleasurable to read.

I can recall very little of what my mother told me about Losice, the city of her birth, where she lived until she was sixteen. In order to enrich my story, I have included in this introduction accounts of life in Losice by former residents who reveal their warm affection for their hometown. The first is a remarkably poetic article attributed to Josef Friedman:

Can We Forget?

Can we forget the mother from whose breast we nursed, or in whose arms we were raised, or in whose hands we saw the first rays of sunlight, or whose lips covered us with warm kisses? So too can we forget the shtetl on whose ground we took our first steps, whose fields and gardens satisfied our hunger, in whose fields, on most memorable spring days we hid in the shadows when the sun was exactly in the middle of the sky, and in whose stormy river we cooled our heated bodies.

Losice was blessed with natural beauty. It was a tiny shtetl encircled by wide, open fields and deep forests. Every field and forest had a name. Every field had different flowers and every forest had different trees.... A special role was played in Losice by the farm *pole nowy* (new field), with its two waterfalls, rapids, and large field surrounded by groves of old poplars. How many happy songs were sung here during the summer months! The songs of Losicer youth mingled with the songs of a variety of birds. Bundists[1] and future leaders would sing songs about work and hardship, songs of freedom and songs about socialism.... How many sweet memories the Losicers carry with them from those years when Yiddishkeit radiated from every corner! Jewish words and songs accompanied us through our youth...there were places known for their intense learning. The light of knowledge shone from these houses....

Our fathers and mothers are not there anymore. Gone are those who cared for us, who would kiss us, who would shudder at every step.... No longer do we have our brothers and sisters, with whom we shared our best years as children and youths, with whom we dreamed and with whom we often thought that in the near, near future a happy morning would dawn for our people. A terrible Nazi storm took everyone. Who knew, who could have imagined, the killings by which all of them, our nearest and dearest, would perish?

---

[1] Bundists were a secular Jewish socialist movement, whose organizational manifestation was the General Jewish Labour Bund in Lithuania, Poland and Russia.

The second is by Chaim Iczel Goldstein, who grew up in Losice during the beginning of the twentieth century. He wrote lovingly about his birthplace, as others who were born there did, in order that the story of Losice would live on after the disaster of the Holocaust that decimated the entire Jewish population. He recounts:

From earliest childhood I remember the large square in the middle of the shtetl. Here market days would take place which were not only lively for the merchants and artisans, but also for the plain folk...When a *yarid* (market day) approached the Jews would end their praying sooner in order to come to the *Rynek* (market location). They would come with empty bags to wait for the farmers to come into town from neighboring villages. The farmers would bring corn, potatoes, sacks of onions, a calf for meat which was tied up behind the market, a young cow to sell, or a skinny cow which had stopped producing milk which was destined to the Jewish butcher's ritual slaughterhouse.

We bought everything the farmers had to offer, and so they earned their poor livelihood. While waiting between one stand and another we were able to chat with each other, a good word from the Rebbe, and a discussion about a Gemara portion which had started the prior evening between *Mincha* and *Maariv* (prayer times). So it was that a little politics of local events was never lacking...The debates would always end on a positive note; words of confidence and hope; God will help us!

In the middle of the square there was a cluster of shops—among them were restaurants, artisan shops, hatmakers, tailors, shoemakers, and two bakeries...It was a short time before the First World War, when the shoemaking industry pulled the shtetl out of its depression.... Factories sprang up, creating work and, in turn, money...From the Notawzne Street...and from behind the synagogue could be heard:

Hammer, Hammer, Clap
Hit harder a nail, another nail,
You are my only means
From hunger, without you, I would die...

That song by Abraham Raizins became an anthem for the shoemakers in Losice.

This description informs us of an aspect of the lives of our parents that was missing from their narrative. It gives us a "sense of place" and a better appreciation of who we are and where we came from.

Although some of the characters in this book are completely fictional, most are based on actual members of my extended family, using their real names. The photographs included are of those real people.

Perhaps it's foolish for me to concern myself about this matter. I'm hopeful this story will be read by many members of the Singer and Binstock families. And after having been read, parts of the tale I have woven will be remembered and shared with other family members. And as often happens, as time passes, the fictional story may evolve into family history. That might be unfortunate or, in the long run…it might not matter at all.

Bill Nemoyten
Hayward, California
March 2018

Acknowledgements

The creation of this book would not have happened without the family research done by my cousin, Dr. Phillip Lerner, when he wrote "Cousins, the Next Generation." I am dedicating this book to his memory. Many of the key events I found in Dr. Lerner's book were those that inspired me to create this story and can be found in Parts Two and Three. Part One of this book came about as a result of information provided by Fred Binstock.

My thankyou goes to my daughter, Jo Nemoyten, for her encouragement and expert work in turning my story into a published book. Her work included selecting and placing photos and designing the cover art. As this book was being written, I read it chapter by chapter to several individuals who listened patiently and further encouraged me to continue and complete my tale. They included the treasured and talented members of my writer's group, Diane Ghostley, Al Murdock and John Steinbach. I also shared the manuscript when reading it to my wife Barbara and her roommate Maxine Freeman at the Bay Point Rehab Center. My other children Mark and David Nemoyten and Susan Cortez gave me encouragement and assistance along the way.

Most of this story is fictional, but it is inspired by my feelings of pride in being a member of the Singer family. There were originally eighteen Singer first cousins, all the grandchildren of Chaim and Dina Singer. I am indebted to my surviving cousins for the information they shared with me. They include Shirley Silver, Jeanette Berman, Donald Singer, Edwin Singer, Dr. Allan Lerner, Burton Saltzman, Deanie Wainstein and Helene Krasney. Information about the Kentucky branch of the Singer family came partially from the son of my cousin Shirley, Paul Levy of Oxfordshire, UK. I'm especially appreciative of the assistance of Edwin Singer in providing the funding for my excellent editor, Teja Watson.

I am further honored to have had the Preface written by Dr. Marilyn Boxer, Emeritus Professor of History, San Francisco State University.

Map showing Losice in Poland

Locise was pronounced *LAW-shts* by my Yiddish-speaking relatives. In Polish, it is pronounced *waw-SHEE-tsa*.

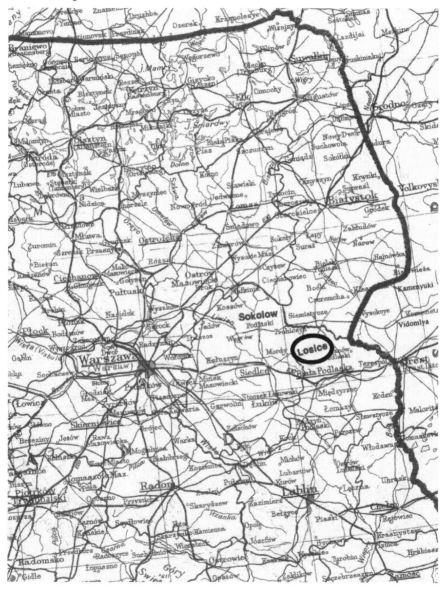

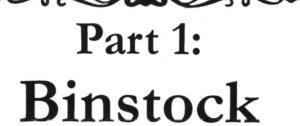

Part 1:
Binstock

Chapter 1

How a Match Was Made

Avrum Binstock had apprenticed as a shoemaker since the age of fourteen. He had been practicing his trade for eight years in the Polish town of Losice, 116.9 kilometers east of Warsaw. Although pictures of him with a stern visage seem to indicate otherwise, Avrum was a friendly and outgoing man. He had a slender, muscular build, dark hair, and a neatly trimmed beard and mustache. The highest status in the Jewish community was certainly not reserved for shoemakers, blacksmiths, or the like, but for the scholars of the holy books: the Torah, the Talmud, and the Gemara. And while Avrum hadn't garnered the respect in his Jewish community that he might have if he had applied himself to his studies of Hebrew, he was contented with his life. One of Avrum's favorite Yiddish proverbs was, *"Nayn rabonim kenen keyn minyen nit makhn ober tsen shusters yo,"* translated as, "Nine rabbis can't make a minyan, but ten shoemakers can." (Ten Jewish men who have had a Bar Mitzvah are required for a *minyan*, needed to conduct certain daily prayers.)

Rather than studying the holy books, Avrum had always enjoyed a deep sense of satisfaction working with his hands. Now he worked with them all day and had become a skilled craftsman, not just at repairing shoes and boots, but also at skillfully working leather into handsome new shoes and boots for men and women. Many Losice families were his customers and he was making a modest but comfortable living.

The year was 1891. Faiga, Avrum's wife of two years, was the sister of the well-known *sofer*[2], Chaim Zynger. Avrum felt very blessed to be connected to the Zynger family. Today he was daydreaming, remembering the wonderful day when his parents told him Chana Rosen, the matchmaker, had approached them about a union between the Binstocks and the Zyngers. Ever since he was a youth—in fact, since his Bar Mitzvah age—he had been charmed by the beautiful Faiga Zynger. At Shabbat services, and the many Jewish holiday celebrations in the town's synagogue, he would slyly steal looks up into the balcony where the women sat, separated from the men, to see if he could catch a glimpse of her. He was enthralled as he gazed at her sweet

---

[2] A sofer is a scribe of the Torah, the five books of Moses or The Old Testament.

face and the grace of her slim figure as she wended her way through the stalls with her mother on market days.

Though Chaim Zynger was widely known and respected for his creation of magnificently scribed Torahs, Chaim's father and the rest of the Zynger family were not very prosperous. They could only offer a small dowry for Faiga. But when Avrum's father balked at the offer, Avrum brushed the dowry issue aside, saying, "I don't need or want a large dowry from the Zyngers. I am confident of my ability to provide for my wife, and dear father, there is no other woman who could make me as happy as Faiga." When Avrum's father saw that pleading look in his son's eyes, he knew he must swallow his pride. He called upon the delighted matchmaker, declaring, "We will have a match. Let's prepare for the *chasanah* (wedding)."

But what of Faiga? How did she feel about the arranged match? That is the way it happened in those days and in that place, as well as in many other places around the world. She was sixteen, an age when many young girls were married, often to much older men. She had known Avrum all of her life and sensed his interest in her. She felt fortunate to be matched with a young, attractive, strong, and healthy man. She understood her role in life was to be a good wife, who would hope to have many children. But she had always felt uncomfortable about the Jewish custom that when a woman was to be married, her hair was to be shaved off and she was required to wear a *scheidle* (wig) from then on. As for sex, she was surprised and puzzled when her mother explained how babies were made, and what would be expected of her by her husband. But, as in all other matters involving essential life cycle events, she trusted in God.

What a wonderful chasanah it was! Faiga was wearing a lovely white gown, sewn by her talented cousin Rebekah. She was nervous but radiant on her wedding day. Avrum, more excited than nervous, wore a new black suit and a handsomely embroidered *kipah* (skullcap). The *ketubah* (marriage contract) was prepared and signed. Rabbi Rubinstein presided over the ceremony. As the young couple stood under the *chuppah* (wedding canopy), Cantor Feldstein, a nasally tenor, chanted the ancient Hebrew words that have united Jewish couples for countless generations. The glass was set on the floor and smashed by the groom, according to tradition, and the *Mazel tovs* were shouted by the assembled throng.

Shot glasses of schnapps were downed by the men and the Losicer klezmer musicians struck up the rollicking *Chasen Kallah Mazel tov*! (Good Luck to the Bride!). The klezmer group was led by an energetic violinist with a schmaltzy vibrato. The band included a wailing clarinetist, a thumping bass fiddle, and a surprisingly talented, very young accordion player, whose fingers flew nimbly over the keyboard. They filled the hall with their rhythmically exuberant melodies. In the orthodox tradition, the men danced with each other, while on the other side of the room divider, the women danced. The food tables sagged under the weight of trays of a *milchedich* (non-meat) menu: noodle kugels, potato knishes, cheese blintzes, pickles, bean salad, smoked white fish, water bagels, twisted raisin and dried fruit-filled challahs, apple strudel, and rugalach.

The party roared on for hours. Then, midnight intruded. The music ended. The tables of food now bore only a few scraps of this and that. The bottles of schnapps were drained of their fire. The guests and their sleepy children vacated the hall with the best of wishes to the bride and groom, the young men leering knowingly at the soon-to-be-united couple. The gifts were carted to the groom's home by his friends, and the happy but overwhelmed couple retired to the wedding chamber.

Avrum's father and his uncle had spoken to him about what should take place on his wedding night. Avrum's hands shook wildly as he began to disrobe. In his excitement, he had forgotten all the advice he had been given. But Faiga, having been mentored by her wise mother, was somehow more calm and composed. She gently guided Avrum in the ways of lovemaking and the marriage was consummated.

Having awakened just before the dawn of the first day of his married life, Avrum tenderly kissed the forehead of his sleeping bride and then lay in bed listening to the gentle sound of her breathing—heaven's most beautiful music. He felt a surge of excitement and exhilaration about how much brighter his future would now be. Then he was overcome by yet another surge: the surge of ambition. As he looked at the lovely face of his wife, Faiga, he resolved to work harder than ever.

It was then, at that moment, that the seed of an idea about how he could build a better life for his family took root in his mind—a dream that would eventually prove to be life-changing not only for him and Faiga, but for so very many others for generations to come.

Chapter 2

The Journey to Warsaw

Avrum thought he was on the threshold of realizing his dream when an unusual opportunity arose. His brother-in-law, Chaim Zynger, after a year of meticulous work, had just completed one of his very finest Torahs. Chaim's reputation as an outstanding sofer had been spreading to other communities and had now reached the influential rabbis in Warsaw. The well-respected Warsaw Rabbi, Hillel Horowitz, had visited his relatives in Mezrich, a town near Losice, where he was given the opportunity to read from a Chaim Zynger Torah in their small synagogue during the Shabbat celebration. He told the local rabbi he had never seen such a beautifully penned Torah and wanted to know who had created the extraordinary scroll. Six months later, having raised the necessary fee to pay for a much-needed new Torah, he had written to Chaim Zynger, commissioning him to create a new one for his Warsaw synagogue. Rabbi Horowitz requested Chaim Zynger deliver the Torah himself when it was completed, if at all possible, because he wanted to honor him at the dedication of the new Torah, which was to be installed in their ark, along with a handsome new silver breastplate, crowns, and pointer.

The 116-kilometer journey to Warsaw in a horse-drawn carriage would take two days. It would be exhausting, and possibly hazardous! Occasionally there had been reports of robberies on isolated parts of the old dirt road. And in addition, there was always the fear of attacks from rabid anti-Semites, who were from time to time goaded into pogroms against Jews by the Catholic clergy. Chaim discussed the pros and cons of the trip with his wife, Dina, and with his sister Faiga and her husband, Avrum. After a lengthy deliberation, during which Avrum argued strongly for the trip and declared that he would accompany Chaim, the decision to proceed with the journey was made.

In addition to helping Chaim, Avrum had his own agenda. He had for some time wanted to travel to Warsaw, as he sensed the key to his dream of improving his life would somehow be discovered in the great city. But he also felt confident he would be able to provide some measure of protection to his scholarly but delicate brother-in-law. Avrum was tall in stature and sturdily built. In addition, he had a reputation for being fearless. Anti-Semitic bullies, who from time to time abused the erudite young Yeshiva students, learned to avoid confrontations with Avrum Binstock, who gave them more than they could handle. On that Monday morning, just as they were about to leave for Warsaw, Avrum ran back into his work room to put a special item into his pocket, an item he was hoping he would not to have to reveal or use during the journey.

It was a clear and sunny day. There was birdsong and a few puffy clouds floating across the blue sky. Thankfully, it hadn't rained for several days, and the road—which was often, during the rainy season, a muddy quagmire— was on that day relatively smooth. All went well for several hours and they were occasionally greeted by other friendly travelers heading toward Losice and other small towns along the way. They spent the first night with some relatives who lived nearer to Warsaw. They were approaching the outskirts of Warsaw late on the second day, when Avrum saw a man standing in the middle of the road a short distance ahead. He approached the man cautiously, sensing trouble.

Gregor Krasky was in an unusually foul mood, brought on by his Polish vodka-induced state of inebriation. His mood was foul because his last bottle was empty, and he had no *kopeks* to secure any more of the fruity alcoholic liquid he required to forget who he was and what an utter mess he had made of his pitiful life. A rail-thin man with a pockmarked face and watery blue eyes, Gregor had managed to alienate everyone in his family by stealing from them to feed his insatiable vodka dependency. Now penniless, all he could think of was finding some way, any way, to get more vodka. He lived in a shack near the old road to Warsaw and considered the idea of robbing passing travelers. But having no weapon and no nerve, he rejected the thought. His alcohol-dazed mind searched for an idea. "Yes," he thought. "I'll find someone who looks weak so they won't give me any trouble. I know what I'll tell them. They will just hand over their money. Gregor, you are such a smart man."

After an hour of waiting beside the road in the hot sun, Gregor spied a carriage approaching. There was a tall man holding the reins of the horse and another man who appeared to be sleeping. They both wore beards and the skullcaps of Jews. Gregor thought, "This will be easy."

As they approached, Avrum was suddenly confronted by the surly-looking stranger he had seen in the middle of the road, who shouted in a gruff voice, "Stop, Jews. You are traveling on my road. You'll have to pay me five rubles!"

Avrum reined in the horse. Chaim, who had been napping, suddenly awoke and asked, "Avrum, what is happening?"

Avrum calmly said, "Don't be concerned. I'll deal with this ruffian."

Turning to the stranger, Avrum said, "This is a public road and belongs to all the people, but if there is something you want, I'll get it for you."

Gregor Krasky rubbed his hands together in anticipation of what he was certain would be an easy way to extract some rubles from travelers from now on. He was already imagining the feel of the money he was about to collect. He pictured a long line of vodka bottles waiting to slake his thirst.

Avrum had a different idea. He reached into his pocket and pulled out the shiny razor-sharp knife he used for cutting leather. He stood up in the wagon, leaned toward the man, and pointed his knife threateningly at the would-be robber. Avrum, looking directly into the eyes of Krasky, shouted, "This is what you will have to deal with if you still think you want those five rubles!"

Startled by Avrum's response, Gregor, seeing the sharp, gleaming blade, was taken by surprise. He shrank back out of the way of the carriage, and with that Avrum snapped the reins. The horse obeyed, taking them quickly down the road as Gregor Krasky swore anti-Semitic curses.

Chapter 3

Discoveries in the Great City

The rest of the trip went well. When they reached the city they found Chaim's cousins, who lived on Krachmalnik Street, eagerly awaiting their arrival. The exhausted men were invited to stay in their modest home. The Torah was delivered and arrangements for the dedication the next day were made with Rabbi Horowitz. It was then that Avrum told Chaim he wanted to walk about and explore the city for a few hours.

While the Industrial Revolution was well underway in America and Warsaw and the other larger cities of Europe, it hadn't yet touched the smaller remote towns like Losice. Avrum was wide-eyed with wonder and amazement as he walked through the crowded streets of downtown Warsaw. At one point, very late in the day, he heard a loud horn followed by a flood of hundreds of men spilling out of the largest building he had ever seen. The men all looked tired and grimy, as if they had been through a long, arduous ordeal. Avrum, seeing that many of them were going into a tavern, followed them and decided to do something he had rarely done in his life: He ordered food in a restaurant, first making certain they had simple food he hoped would not violate Jewish dietary laws. He ordered eggs, boiled potatoes, and beet borscht. As he ate, Avrum strained to hear what the noisy beer-drinking workers were talking about. One of the men looked at him suspiciously, then turned to another man and made a comment to his friend about the stranger. They both laughed and went back to their beer mugs.

Avrum, as he listened to the discussions, gathered that the men were unhappy about how they were treated in the large building where they worked. The building was a factory where furniture was made, and they made so much of it that it was loaded onto railroad cars whose tracks led right up to the side of the building. That was a revelation to Avrum, because, until that moment, as far as he knew, furniture was always made by individual craftsmen and their apprentices.

After the meal, Avrum, exuberant with the flood of new experiences, turned a corner and was astounded by what came into view next. Moving down Iron Street and filled with passengers was the longest carriage he had ever seen, but to his utter astonishment there were no horses pulling it. Its wheels were running on what looked like railroad tracks, and there were wires overhead mysteriously connected to poles on the roof of the carriage. He was soon to learn that he had seen one of the first electrically powered trolley cars in Warsaw.

Next, Avrum explored a street with many stores, including some that sold only shoes and boots. He examined the footwear carefully and noted that though the quality was no better than the shoes he himself made, the merchants were charging three times as much as he did in Losice. Avrum was getting more excited by the moment. Ideas were cascading through his mind so fast he was nearly dizzy. He thought of all the things he must do and visualized exactly how he would accomplish them. The morning following the dedication of the new Torah, Avrum was bursting with energy and enthusiasm. He exclaimed to Chaim, "We must return to Losice as soon as we can. I have so much to do."

Chapter 4

Seeking Advice

Before they left Warsaw, Avrum spoke to a Mr. Petrof, a neighbor of Chaim's cousins. A kindly man, Petrof was willing to share what he knew about the coat factory where he worked. Avrum wanted to know precisely how the factory functioned. Petrof explained how mass production worked—how each person had one task to perform, such as cutting material or sewing on buttons. He then passed the item he was working on to the next person, who did something else to the coat. He explained how efficient the system was and bragged about the enormous number of coats manufactured at the factory each day.

Avrum thought about what Petrof had said for a few minutes and then said, "But if each person is doing the same thing all day long, over and over again, don't they get tired and bored?"

"Yes, that's true for some people, but everyone is happy to have a job they can count on and money to help feed their families."

Avrum nodded in understanding. He wanted more information, and Petrof seemed to enjoy sharing with the eager young man from the small town. They spent two hours together, Avrum writing everything down in a small notebook.

The trip home was uneventful, but seemed to Avrum to go on forever, because of his yearning to get started. Shabbat was approaching, and they had to reach Losice before dinner time to prepare for Shabbat. When he should have been praying, Avrum's mind was instead running over his plans for the next day and the many days to come.

Faiga—as a special treat, because she was so happy to have her husband and brother return home safely—prepared a plate of delicious cheeses blintzes for Avrum, his absolute favorite. After he filled his belly with them, Avrum told Faiga about all he had seen in Warsaw. As he sipped a cup of hot tea, he revealed his plan to her.

He said, "I intend to open a shoe factory right here in our own home. I hope you are agreeable to that idea." He said, "I will have to borrow money to get started. It will be for tools, work tables, leather...all kinds of things. We will probably soon have to expand our home." He told the overwhelmed Faiga all he had learned about mass production and said, "I will find workers and teach each one how to do a different part of the shoe, until they have become experts at their tasks. Then the shoes will be stitched and nailed together, under my supervision. When enough are finished we will load them on a wagon…." Avrum stopped to make a note. "Yes, a wagon," he said. "I will need a large wagon and a good horse, to take my shoes to Warsaw. I'll sell them there and use the money to buy more supplies."

Faiga stood, flabbergasted. She declared, "My husband, I had no idea you had such great aspirations. I want you to know I love you and believe in you. But where will you get the money to buy all those things?"

"I don't know. I have been thinking about who I should ask for advice. I think I'll start by asking the rabbi." In small towns such as Losice Jews greatly respected their rabbi, who was the most educated person they knew, even though their education was entirely based on their knowledge of the Torah, Talmud, and the other holy books, and had little to do with the problems of daily life.

Avrum wrote out his plan, including what he thought would be the cost of each item. Next, he went to see Rabbi Rubinstein, whom he considered to be a very wise man. Perhaps the rabbi would have some ideas about how he could go about raising the money. But he also wanted to hear what the rabbi thought about his idea. Rabbi Rubinstein had known him all his life. The rabbi, who was also a *mohel*, had performed his ritual circumcision. The rabbi had been his *cheder* (Hebrew school) teacher, had officiated at his Bar Mitzvah and at his wedding.

The *Rebbitzen* (rabbi's wife), Leah, answered the door, and greeting him warmly she asked, "Nu Avrum, what brings you to see the rabbi? I hope it's good news. Is there soon going to be a new little Binstock?"

Blushing, Avrum replied, "Not as far as I know, Mrs. Rubinstein. Is the rabbi in, and do you think he can see me now?"

"Yes, Avrum, he is at home. Come, sit down at the kitchen table, where he is having his afternoon tea. Can I get a cup for you? How many lumps of sugar do you like?"

"Thank you. That would be very nice. Three, please."

The aging rabbi, with his flowing white beard, peered over the book he was reading with his twinkling eyes and smiled broadly as Avrum entered the room.

"Come, sit down, Avrum. So tell me, what brings you here to see me in the middle of the day? Is there a problem in the Binstock house? Is Faiga alright?"

Avrum sat down at the table. Dropping the three cubes of sugar in his tea, he thought about what he would say to this wise old man, who had been so much a part of his life for so many years.

"Rabbi," he began, "everything is good at the Binstock house, and my shoemaking business is good as well. I came to you for advice. An idea has taken hold of me. It is a dream I have. Rabbi, I'm just a shoemaker, but I want to become more than that. I know I can make and operate a shoemaking factory right here in Losice. I have made all the plans, but I need money…a lot of money, to get started. I don't know how people do that…how they get the money to start a business."

"Well, well, Avrum, I must tell you, you have surprised me. I had no idea you were a man of such great ambition. If you had a question about a passage in the Torah or the Talmud I would gladly try to help you, but you need the advice of a businessman, not a rabbi. Let me think…ah, yes, you should see Herschel Herzog. He is the most successful businessman in Losice. If anyone can advise you, it's Reb Herzog. Please give my greetings to Faiga."

With that said, the rabbi turned back to his book. Avrum rose and said good-bye to the rabbi and the Rebbitzen and headed toward the Herzog home, satisfied he had gotten good advice from the rabbi.

Avrum had seen Herzog at the synagogue from time to time, but he had never spoken to him, feeling he was not in Reb Herzog's social class. In fact, he felt intimidated by the portly and finely dressed rich merchant, with his large-bosomed wife and elegant horse and carriage. On the day of his visit he gathered his courage and knocked on the merchant's door, feeling fortified by the fact that Rabbi Rubinstein had referred him to Herzog. The servant, Yankel Lewinski, a man he knew slightly, came to the door. It was the first time Avrum had ever been to a home that employed a servant.

Avrum greeted Yankel with the traditional "Shalom Aleichem, Yankel. Is Reb Herzog at home? Rabbi Rubinstein told me I should come to see him."

Just then, before Yankel had a chance to respond, Herschel Herzog came into the room. Herzog had accumulated great wealth by Losice standards, but unfortunately, because of his wealth, he had also acquired an arrogant, overbearing attitude and an undisguised air of patronizing superiority.

He began by declaring, "You are the shoemaker Binstock, aren't you? What business do you have with me? I take care of my shoe needs on my frequent trips to Warsaw."

"Well, you see, Reb Herzog, I spoke to Rabbi Rubinstein about my plan to start a new business and he told me that you could advise me."

Still standing near the doorway, instead of inviting Avrum into his home, Herzog responded saying, "Did you say 'start a business'? I thought you repaired shoes. That's your business, isn't it?"

"Well, sir, you see, I have this plan."

"Plan? What plan can a shoemaker have?"

At the imperious, disdainful way Herzog was treating him, Avrum, who ordinarily possessed a calm and reserved nature, felt a surge of resentment and anger building within him. He had approached the merchant humbly, merely seeking advice, and was being treated with contempt. His ambition was powerful and he felt he had nothing to lose by asserting himself at this moment.

"Reb Herzog," he began slowly, with a level of conviction so strong he surprised himself. "Yes, I am just a shoemaker, but a very good shoemaker, and like any other man I have a desire to improve my place in this world. I plan to start a shoemaking factory here in Losice."

Herzog laughingly spouted, "A factory here in Losice? You, a shoemaker? What do you know about factories? You're making a joke, aren't you?"

"No, this is not a joke. I know enough about how factories work and I know a great deal about making shoes. What I need to know more about is money."

"A-ha!" bellowed Herzog. "That's what you came about. Everyone is always trying to get money from me one way or another. I'm not foolish enough to give my money to a shoemaker. Think of it—what foolishness, a shoemaking factory in Losice!"

Avrum, clenching his fists in an attempt to control his anger, retorted, "Reb Herzog, I came to you for advice, not for money. There are others who will understand my plan and I will open a shoemaking factory here in Losice. Good day."

With his chin held high, he strode out the door. Avrum, though he had been insulted and laughed at by the merchant, experienced a new sense of his own power, formerly unknown to him. He had stood up to the mocking words of Herzog with strength and audacity.

Chapter 5

Dina to the Rescue

After his meeting with Herschel Herzog, Avrum set about raising the money he needed with more determination than ever. He harbored a wish that the day would come when the pompous Herzog would go to Warsaw to buy shoes, bring them back and boast about how fine they were, and then learn, much to his chagrin, that they were made in Binstock's shoe factory right here in Losice.

But Avrum also had doubts. While he knew all about how to work leather—how to cut it, how to fashion a fine shoe or boot, and how to dye the leather expertly—he knew little about raising money and financing a business. When Avrum sat down with Faiga to discuss what he would do next, the first idea that came into her mind was to consult her sister-in-law, Dina. That was not surprising. Dina was, by necessity, a very clever and enterprising woman. She was the mother of a growing family whose husband was a highly respected sofer who wrote magnificent Torahs. But being the scribe of the Pentateuch, even the very best of scribes, was no guarantee of financial security. He made a little money teaching a few students and writing the tiny Mezuzah scrolls. But it took a whole year to complete a Torah and often he wasn't paid fully for his effort immediately but had to wait several months.

Dina loved her husband very deeply and appreciated his unique talent. But she had a household to maintain and her husband's income was not sufficient. So, she used her ingenuity to bring in more money. She walked out to nearby farms, assisted by her children, bought produce, and sold it to her neighbors. She was also skilled with needle and thread and made clothing for her family. She was always on the lookout for opportunities to make or save money. As a result, she had not only succeeded in keeping up the family standard of living but had accumulated money for an anticipated "rainy day."

Avrum had great respect for Dina and agreed to ask her for advice. When Avrum and Faiga arrived at the home of Reb Chaim Zynger they were greeted warmly by everyone, especially the children. Avrum always brought them some kind of treat. This time it was dried fruit to chew on and hard candies to suck on.

Chaim, Dina, Faiga, and Avrum sat down around the kitchen table. The air in the room was heavy with the sweet smell of challah baking in the oven and the not-so-sweet odor of gefilte fish boiling in a big pot on the wood stove. Dina had filled the shiny brass Samovar with water and had put out glasses for tea, along with her delicious crunchy *mandel broit* (similar to biscotti). After chatting a while about their families, the synagogue, and preparations for the next Jewish holiday of Purim, Avrum began by telling the story of his plan to start his own shoe factory in Losice and the way the trip to Warsaw revealed clearly what he must do. He even told about how his attempt to get advice from Reb Herzog was rebuffed, and finally why he had come to them for advice.

Chaim commented to Dina, saying, "You have engaged in business, a world unknown to me. Do you think Avrum's idea is a good one?"

Dina nodded. "Avrum, tell us more about what you plan to do and how we can help you."

After Avrum described what his shoe factory would look like and how it would work, Dina asked him how much money he would need to get started. He answered, "I have a little money of my own, but I will need another two hundred rubles to get started."

Dina drank some tea and then she started to tap her index finger on the table, a habit they all knew meant she was engaged in serious thinking. After a couple more minutes, Dina looked up at Avrum and asked, "If we or our friends or relatives would lend you money, what could we expect in return?"

Avrum was ready with his answer. "There are three ways I could repay them: with money, with shoes, or by giving them or their sons' jobs."

"How much money, Avrum?"

"For every twenty rubles they lent me for a year I would pay them one ruble. For those who could only lend me a few rubles, I would pledge to give them shoes and boots. And I expect, at the beginning, to employ five or six young men, who would earn money to help their families."

"That's a good answer, Avrum," Dina declared. And then she said, "Give me a few days to think about this."

After the meeting, Avrum didn't know quite what to think. What idea could Dina have that he hadn't already thought about? Just as he had done several times before, he went to his secret hiding place. In a jar hidden in a corner of the family's root cellar, behind a large barrel, was a leather pouch with his life savings.

Once again, he counted it. And once again, he came to the conclusion that he needed much more money to get his factory started.

A day passed, then another and another, without any word from Dina. As Avrum continued to work at his bench each day, he became more frustrated and discouraged. He felt awkward about asking his customers to lend him money. Nevertheless, he did approach a few of them, four of whom lent him a few rubles, but nowhere what was needed.

Chapter 6

Avrum, the Salesman

It was the morning after the fun holiday of Purim. The doughy three-cornered poppy seed-filled Hamentachen were all eaten and Faiga had just finished putting the costumes for the beautiful Queen Esther and wicked Hamen away for another year.

Faiga heard some voices outside and suddenly there was a knock on the door. It was Dina, wearing a big, self-satisfied smile on her face. She was accompanied by several neighbors. Faiga greeted warmhearted old Mr. and Mrs. Feigenbaum; the always cheerful Chana Rosenberg; the wealthy Cohens, Beryl and Sarah; and the red-bearded Leibowitz twins, Yitzchak and Benjamin.

As they stepped into the house, Dina declared, "We've come to talk business with Avrum."

There was no sleeping for Avrum that night. Though he was tired from all that had happened that day, his body and mind were charged with the excitement of what lay ahead. There was so much to think and dream about. First, he would have to go to the homes of the people Dina had brought to his home. Although he explained his shoe factory plan to the group, it would be necessary to call on each of them in their own homes. They would not want the others to know how much money they had invested. Avrum would need to reinvent himself as a salesman, a skill he had never been taught.

He chose the path of least resistance by starting with Dov and Chana Feigenbaum, both in their late sixties and old friends of his family. If there was anyone he felt comfortable talking to, it was the Feigenbaums, who were those rare individuals who seem to be perpetually sweet, warm-hearted, and happy with their lot in life. As he entered their warm and welcoming home, a home that reflected their personalities to perfection, Chana Feigenbaum planted a kiss on Avrum's cheek and invited him to have a cup of tea and a homemade water bagel spread with *schmaltz* (rendered chicken fat).

Avrum's sales talk was brief because the Feigenbaums had already made up their minds to help him. Dov went into their bedroom and withdrew twenty rubles from his secret hiding place. When Avrum offered them a written promise to pay the money back with interest, Dov waved the offer away, saying, "We trust you as if you were our own son. We wish you and Faiga well. You'll repay us whenever you can."

Lifted by the warmth of his first sales encounter, in the next few days Avrum called on the others that Dina had brought to his home. Then, as the word spread in the Jewish community, others inquired, and Avrum visited many more homes in the ensuing days. In a month he had raised more than he'd originally hoped for and was ready for his next step.

Chapter 7

Nightmare

Shabbat was ending. As always, Avrum and Faiga planned to walk to the synagogue to participate in the *Ma-ariv* (afternoon) service. Avrum, who been working six days a week at his trade, eating a quick dinner, and then going out each cold night to raise money, was exhausted. He knew Faiga enjoyed visiting with the other women after the service, though, so he didn't tell her how he was feeling.

As was the custom, Rabbi Rubinstein waited until it was dark to look at the heavens outside, to discover if Shabbat had officially ended so he could lead the Havdalah end of Shabbat service. It could only begin when three stars could be seen at the same time in the night sky in a single glance.

Avrum remembered that what happened next occurred right after Havdalah. The entwined candle had been dipped in the wine and "Eliahu Hanovi" had been sung, ending the service. It was then that Avrum felt an ominous chill surge through his body. Faiga was socializing with the women and didn't notice how pale he had become.

Avrum sat down in a corner of the synagogue, his head swimming. Most of the congregants had left. Faiga and some of the women were still talking when Rabbi Rubinstein noticed Avrum sitting alone, looking pale and sickly. Avrum attempted to stand and greet the rabbi, but fell back in the chair, the room swimming about him in a dizzying circle.

The alarmed rabbi called to Faiga and some of the men still in the building. Avrum was given some of the sweet ritual wine to drink. It didn't help. He was suddenly too weak to walk without help. A carriage was brought to the door and Avrum was helped into it.

That night Avrum shivered uncontrollably for several hours, while Faiga covered him with blankets and warmed the house. She built a large fire in their wood stove. Later Avrum became very warm, then very hot, running a high fever.

In a half-awake, half-asleep delirium he had a dream. He was in a strange place. It was an enormous room with huge windows providing light for a row of benches and work tables lined up in rows, stretching as far as the eye could see. There were workmen at each table, all working on shoes. As they worked they were chanting the "Kaddish," the traditional memorial prayer written in the ancient language of Aramaic. The mournful chant was sung in a slow, dirge-like manner, as if they were at a funeral.

In his dream he was floating about freely. He moved effortlessly through the enormous room until he came to what appeared to be an office. He read the large lettering on the door: "The Herschel Herzog Shoe Company." In very small, nearly unreadable badly worn letters below were the words, "Formerly The Binstock Shoe Company."

Avrum awoke, startled. He sat up in bed and called to Faiga. She came running into the room.

"What is it, Avrum? What's the matter?"

He shared his chilling dream with her in agitated short bursts of words that left his mouth with great difficulty, as if it was filled with food he kept chewing but couldn't swallow.

Faiga tried to calm him, saying, "Avrum, my darling, you must rest and save your strength." She was distraught. It appeared that Avrum had the dreaded influenza, a disease that was often fatal. Avrum laid back down in a miserable state, unable to sleep, unable to feel relief of any kind as his fever raged on. Not knowing what else to do, Faiga brought Avrum a small bowl of chicken soup. He sipped two spoonfuls and shook his head. Later, still burning with fever, Avrum rose again, this time asking for a bucket. He vomited.

The next day Dr. Rostov examined Avrum, shaking his head as he listened to Avrum's labored breathing and feeling his feverish head. He made a few recommendations to Faiga about ways to keep Avrum comfortable, but the last thing he said as he left was, "Ask the rabbi to say a prayer for him."

Chapter 8

Life Is Good

The news of Avrum's illness quickly spread through the Jewish community. Soon friends and relatives were bringing food to Faiga, to show their love and concern and to relieve her of the burden and expense of preparing meals.

Avrum's fever raged on. In his few lucid moments he brooded over the ironic twist of fate that had thrust this terrible sickness upon him just as he was about to achieve his goal. He had begun to believe that, like others he had seen succumb to influenza, he would soon die. But in his fleeting stronger moments he reached down to the depths of his soul, determined to fight for his life with every ounce of energy and courage he could command.

On the fifth day of his ordeal Dr. Rostov visited again. After examining Avrum he confided to Faiga that if the fever didn't break soon, all hope would be gone. Faiga took her place on a chair next to her husband's bed that night, tears blinding her eyes. Avrum slept a fitful sleep as Faiga sobbed out the words: "Please, God, don't take him away from me; not now, not ever."

For the past two months, at her usual time of the month, Faiga had gone to the *Mikveh* (ritual bath house) to regain her purity by immersion in the water—even though no blood had flowed from her. And now she knew why. She had sensed it and now was certain.

She thought, "I have felt life growing in me. Our child will need a father, and Avrum will be a wonderful father." She prayed continuously for his recovery, finally falling asleep in the early morning.

Just before sun-up she awoke, surprised as she felt something touch her arm. It was Avrum's hand. His touch felt cool, strong, and firm. She opened her eyes wide, trying to peer through the darkness. Reaching out with her trembling hand, she felt the sweat-soaked sheet. Then, touching Avrum's body, she knew it: the fever had broken. She cried out, "Oh, Avrum, my love, you have returned to me!" She kept repeating the words "Praise God" as she sobbed uncontrollably.

It was another ten days before Avrum marshalled enough strength to return to his work bench. His narrow escape from death had changed him in ways he could never have imagined. The first day he stepped out into the sunshine was thrilling. He felt a staggering sense of joy in every fiber of his body. Everywhere the colors, the sounds, and the smells were more intense than he had ever known. He gazed at Faiga, who now, with child, became the most beautiful woman in the world. He joyfully greeted everyone on the street, whether he knew them or not. Avrum took a renewed pleasure in his work and his skill improved dramatically. He awoke every morning with the wonderful realization he was a very fortunate and happy man. And furthermore, he had the money he needed to move ahead with his plan. "Oh, my God," he thought, "life is so good!"

Avrum was ready. His plans were all laid out. He gathered together all the money he had received from his investors. Next, he created a detailed list of the tools and supplies he would need to get started with six apprentice/workers. He knew exactly what he would teach each person to do and where in his shop and home they would be situated.

He planned to visit the shoe purveyors in Warsaw and observe what kinds of shoes people preferred to buy and how much they paid for them. Avrum's friend Yakov Rothenberg was the biggest, most impressively brawny young man in the Jewish community—the man everyone called upon for big jobs requiring sheer strength. Rothenberg had never been to Warsaw and quickly agreed to go along on the trip as a companion on the long and possibly perilous journey.

Avrum had learned of the death of a man in a nearby town, whose widow wanted to sell their fine horse and wagon. He bought it, knowing it would be needed for each of his many trips in the years to come. Filled with anticipation and excitement, Avrum awoke before dawn, loaded his wagon, and picked up a sleepy Yakov on his way out of town. What he was to experience in the coming months would have a profound effect on Avrum— an effect beyond his ambitions as a businessman.

Chapter 9

Boris Levinson

On his very first reconnaissance visit to Warsaw, Avrum encountered a man who would eventually have a powerful and far-reaching influence upon him. He met many new men in connection with his business dealings, but none as intelligent or world-wise as Boris Levinson, who, in addition to being a shrewd businessman and purveyor of fine leathers, was a poet and philosopher.

Boris had strikingly dark, almost jet-black hair, and a long, narrow beard that suggested the appearance of one of the prophets in the Torah. At their very first business meeting Levinson took a special interest in the ambitious young Binstock. At first he just wanted to show him the ropes of doing business in Warsaw and teach him who to steer clear of. He knew the unscrupulous Warsaw characters who preyed upon inexperienced, unsuspecting visitors from Poland's smaller towns. In a short time Boris and Avrum developed a genuine friendship.

It was on a cold October night following Yom Kippur services that Boris invited Avrum to his home to break the fast. Avrum met Mrs. Levinson and their five energetic children; the three pre-teen boys all sported curly black hair under their yarmulkes and the two older girls had blond tresses. Basha Levinson prepared a hearty traditional meal of *gefilte* fish (chopped and boiled fish made with eggs, matzo meal, carrots, and spices, served cold with freshly ground horseradish), chicken soup with noodles, baked chicken and *tzimmes* (baked carrots, sweet potatoes prunes, orange juice, cinnamon, honey and salt). Apple- and nut-filled strudel served with tea and honey was the dessert. After the meal, while Basha and her two daughters cleared the table and washed the dishes, Boris and Avrum retired to the parlor, where Boris warmed the room, lighting the ornate fireplace. They began a conversation.

"Thank you for the wonderful meal. Your wife is a marvelous cook. The tzimmes was the best I ever tasted."

Lighting his pipe, Boris declared, "You are most welcome, Avrum. I'm glad you were able to come tonight. We have had many business conversations, but we haven't had a chance to really talk about other important things."

A questioning look on his face, Avrum asked, "What important things do you want to talk about?"

"Have you ever heard of the Haskalah?"

"Yes, I have. Rabbi Rubinstein back in Losice warned us about it, but he never really explained what it was we had to fear."

"I'll tell you what it is, Avrum, and you can decide for yourself whether it is something to fear or embrace." Taking a bottle out of a big oak cabinet with intricately carved doors, Boris offered, "Here, have a sip of Slivovitz and I'll tell you all about the Haskalah. It all started with the famous German philosopher, Moses Mendelssohn. He was a brilliant man who was highly respected. *Haskalah* means enlightenment or education. He said that Jews should open their minds to the outside world and become members of the whole society. He saw the benefits in interacting with the gentile world by gaining a broad education that isn't limited exclusively to knowledge of the Torah, the Talmud, and the Mishnah."

Avrum took his very first sip of the potent plum brandy and felt its heat. Setting his glass aside, he said, "Yes, Boris, that sounds very interesting but what does it have to do with me?"

"Avrum, you are now a businessman. You must deal with many people, some Jews, some gentiles, and yes, some anti-Semites. You need to understand what the larger world is all about in order to deal intelligently with everyone. You have come from a shtetl where your rabbi is the arbitrator in all disputes among you and your Jewish neighbors. But if you have a dispute in Warsaw, you will be dealing with lawyers and government magistrates. The reason your Rabbi Rubinstein warned you about the Haskalah is because he fears the loss of his power in his community."

"So, Boris, tell me, how can I become a more enlightened person? What should I do?"

"Ah," Boris said, "you have already crossed the threshold because you asked that question. Come have another drink, my friend, and I will show you how to play chess, a game that will lead you to enlightenment."

This is a good place in our story to explain why during the nineteenth century many Jews were attracted to the Enlightenment. There are two main divisions of Judaism: the Sephardim, largely from Spain, and the Ashkenazim from Eastern Europe. In both cases, if they were totally observant, their lives were dominated by the rules and regulations set forth in the *Torah* (The Five Books of Moses), also known as the Old Testament, and by the 613 commandments that set forth all the rules.

Traditional Judaism is patriarchal. There are many rules that discriminate against women. Women are not permitted to pray with the men but are separated, required to sit in the balcony of a

synagogue. In the case of divorce, the procedure required is humiliating for the woman. In orthodox congregations, women may not become rabbis and may not read from the Torah. (Women, could not become rabbis, even in the Reform Movement, until 1972.)

For both men and women, life is highly structured. There are prayers that must be recited for a great many activities, morning, afternoon, and evenings. The Sabbath and all holidays must be observed completely. What's left over in time is used to make a living. Those who practice a totally observant life have little real freedom or time to engage in the activities of the larger society.

Chapter 10

The Factory Opens

Avrum returned to Losice with his load of tools and materials, ready to start his factory. He gathered together the six young men who were to be his first employees. They helped him unload the heavily burdened wagon.

Avrum and all his helpers were very excited. There were oohs and aahs when they opened the boxes of fine new tools and sheets of supple leathers. Everyone worked very hard that day and on into the night, setting up the work benches and getting organized. Finally, at ten, Avrum told his exhausted young crew to go home. He continued to work until well past midnight, dropping into bed an exhausted but happy man.

Over the course of the next two months Avrum worked like never before in his life, but with a sense of purpose that drove him to accomplish more than he ever dreamed possible. He was dismayed when he found that three of his apprentices had made many mistakes that he would have to correct. To compound the problem, all three of them were the sons of families who had lent him money to start the business.

However, the other three showed great promise. Among them, that was especially true of his nephew, Israel Zynger. Israel not only showed skill as a cutter of leather, but expressed interest in all phases of the business, often staying around after the others had left, offering any help his uncle might need.

A sturdy, stocky young man, Israel was the son of Avrum's brother-in-law, Chaim Zynger, who was highly trained in Jewish ritual. His father had hopes that his eldest son would have inherited his amazing talent as a scribe; perhaps Israel might even become a rabbi someday. But Israel was a restless young man who had tired of spending long hours at *cheder* (religious school) doing nothing but studying Torah and Talmud day and night. He sensed his future lay in other endeavors he had yet to discover. He thought working for his uncle in his new enterprise might be the first step in a new direction for him.

By experimenting with the different task assignments, Avrum discovered which jobs could be handled by which employees. Some were good at cutting, some with sewing, some with dyeing, some with nailing, some with gluing. Finally, by the tenth week, he felt he had enough good merchandise to show to the stores in Warsaw. He knew it was essential that he make an excellent impression in his first contacts with the merchants of Warsaw. He eliminated several pairs of shoes and boots that weren't in every way as perfect as possible.

As he contemplated his next trip and thought about meeting with his new friend Boris Levinson, Avrum began to be overcome with conflicting feelings. He was fascinated by Boris's revelations of a new way for Jews to encounter the changing world, but he felt the irrepressible pull of his orthodox upbringing. He had been like all the others in the Jewish community: He led a strictly structured life. He knew what was expected of him practically every hour of the day. There was the synagogue and all of his family friends who prayed there together with him. There was the beauty of the Shabbat and the holidays. And most important, there were the traditions that had bound together the community for generations.

At the same time, he was growing increasingly excited about the ideas Boris had introduced to him. But there was no one in Losice he could talk to about those ideas. There were many nights when he had trouble falling asleep. He would lie in bed, staring at the ceiling, thinking about the ideas Boris had discussed with him.

Faiga began to notice the change in him. She tried to get him to talk about what was troubling him, but he resisted. She would be having their first child soon and he didn't want to worry her.

Avrum prepared for his first sales trip to Warsaw. He was excited and nervous about the prospect of selling his shoes and boots and beginning to make what he was hoping and expecting to be a good profit. But he was also looking forward to spending more time with Boris, his new friend and mentor of business and all things worldly. Israel would be invited to come along to assist him. But before they left, Avrum called Israel aside and had a talk with him.

"Israel," he said, "I'm very pleased to have you accompany me to Warsaw. I know you have never been there before. You will find it very exciting and educational. In addition to the business we will be doing you will meet my friend Boris Levinson. He will be sharing his knowledge, not only about business, but about life in Warsaw, other great cities, and even America. He will be talking about the Haskalah as well. I will explain some of that to you along the way, but you would be wise to keep that part of your new knowledge to yourself. Do you understand?"

"Yes, Uncle, I understand. I am very grateful to you for taking me with you. I have dreamed of going to Warsaw and all my life I have wanted to learn more about the world outside of Losice. Thank you for your trust in me. If there is a secret you wish me to keep, I will keep it!"

Chapter 11

Enlightenment

On the trip to Warsaw Avrum and Israel met with Boris: again, first to do business, and then what turned out to be further mentoring by Boris on the subject of the Haskala. Boris was determined to open up Avrum's mind to the greater possibilities available in life. He purchased several tickets for a play at the Yiddish Theatre: *Decktuch,* by a favorite writer of his, [3]Abraham Baer Gottlober.

Abraham Baer
Gottlober

Neither Avrum nor Israel had ever been to a Yiddish theater and were pleased and excited to be invited to join four of the Levinsons. They were dazzled by the costumes and the set, but most impressed by the story and the skill of the actors. Afterward, the party went to a nearby café and Avrum peppered Boris with questions.

"Who is this man Gottlober who wrote that play? Where is he from? How can he know so much about people that he can put the right words in their mouths, and especially funny words?"

"Avrum, he is a brilliant man who is one of the leaders of the Haskala. He has a mind that could not be held captive by old ideas and religious practices that made no sense to him."

"Where was he from? Is he still alive? Tell me more about him."

"His is an interesting story. He was born in Volhynia in 1810 and started out as an ardent Hasidic Jew. He even studied the Kabbalah with the Zohar, the book of Jewish Mysticism.

"Gottlober was married at age fourteen to the daughter of a very pious Jew. The young couple, who were very much in love, had a son. But after Gottlober took a trip with his father to Galicia he came under the influence of a man named Joseph Perl, a great advocate of the Haskala. When he

---

[3] Abraham Bear Gottlober was the great grandfather of this author.

returned, his father-in-law, who was violently opposed to his secular studies, compelled young Abraham to divorce his wife. Understandably, he was embittered by the affair and developed a deep hostility toward orthodoxy, which found satiric expression in his writings."

Avrum asked, "What else has he written?"

"A great deal: other plays, articles, essays, and many poems. Here is one of my favorites, 'The Apple Orchard.'

> Oh come with me, my maiden fair
> Enchant these orchards with its echo
> Through orchards filled with apples red,
> Warm them with your flashing eyes
> Taste this luscious fruit I offer
> And breathe this perfumed morning air,
> Apples sweet as they can be
> Now filled with dew whence shadows fled.
> Precious jewels of earthly coffer
> Come and send your laughter mellow
> One for you and one for me
> Tinkling to the silken skies
> Ah, golden world of make believe
> If you were happy, gay carefree
> Come help this dream fantastic weave
> A dream for you, a dream for me!

Avrum was enchanted by the poem and the wonderful play he had seen. He felt that somehow his life had changed forever that evening.

Chapter 12

Time Passes

Over the next several years the Binstock shoemakers became the Binstock Shoe Company. By the year 1900 it had expanded into a large building at the edge of Losice and had twenty-two workers. Avrum routinely took his trips to Warsaw twice a month and, in addition, stopped to sell his shoes in some of the small towns along the way. He became prosperous and his family had grown. Faiga presented him with a handsome son and four beautiful daughters, and another child was on the way.

While his mind had been expanded into the secular world of Warsaw, Avrum still clung to his Jewish orthodoxy at home. For the first time he had enough money to enable him to donate substantial sums to the synagogue. He was rewarded with a seat close to the eastern wall (symbolizing facing in the direction of Jerusalem, Judaism's holiest city) and honored on the Sabbath with an *Aliyah* on several occasions (the Hebrew prayers chanted before and after the weekly reading of the Torah portion).

Over the course of those years Avrum trained many young men in leather-working. Four of the brighter, more ambitious ones started their own companies. It seemed as if, almost overnight, leather-working became the major industry in Losice. In addition to shoe and boot-making, the industries included furriers and manufacturers of luggage. In fact, leather-working saved the town during the difficult economic times prior to World War I.

Israel, Avrum's nephew, had become his right-hand man, serving as shop foreman when he was away. Israel also accompanied Avrum on many of his trips to Warsaw and came under the influence of Boris Levinson. But, true to his word, he kept that part of his visits to Warsaw a secret from his family and friends.

Because he was so well established in his community, although he had a yearning to see more of the world, particularly America, Avrum never considered moving from Losice. Life for Avrum's family remained stable until the 1940s.

As we will see in the forthcoming chapters, Avrum's help made it possible for his nephew Israel Zynger to enjoy a life of amazing adventures. And now we turn to the life of Israel Zynger.

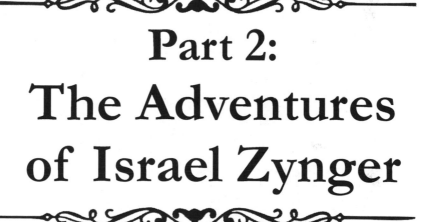

Part 2:
The Adventures
of Israel Zynger

Chapter 13

Israel Moves On

There were three main influences that changed the life of Israel Zynger. The first occurred on a wintry Shabbat in the year 1905. Everyone in the Zynger home was up early that morning; Israel was now seventeen years old. The family had just finished their breakfast of soft-boiled eggs, challah, and tea. They were bundling up in their warmest clothing on a bitterly cold and snowy day, getting ready to trudge to the synagogue against a roaring winter wind for the Shabbat service.

Suddenly shouts and wailing were heard, coming from the direction of their next-door neighbors, the Rosenbaums. As Jews living in the Pale of Settlement, they never felt completely safe. There was always the fear of pogroms, and that is what first came to their minds when they heard the commotion next door. Chaim, Israel's father, motioned to the family to be quiet.

He said, "I will find out what is wrong. Everyone just be calm. Israel, put on your coat and boots quickly and come with me. We will be back as soon as we find out what is happening."

The sounds coming from the Rosenbaum home grew louder and more intense. At first there was just the shouting, but then there was the unmistakable sound of Leah Rosenbaum crying and Zvei Rosenbaum shouting.

Chaim opened his front door, and he and Israel rushed to their longtime neighbor's house. Suddenly the door to the Rosenbaum's home burst open. Two tall, burly Polish soldiers came out of the house with sixteen-year-old Beryl Rosenbaum between them.

The frightened Beryl looked puny next to the two soldiers. He knew he was being conscripted into the dreaded Polish army. He was trying to be brave but was given away by the tears flowing from his eyes, freezing on his bony cheeks. His father was pleading with the soldiers to wait while he brought out a warm coat for his son.

The mustachioed taller of the soldiers growled, "Very well, but hurry up, old man. Don't worry, we'll take good care of your Jew boy." Both soldiers laughed.

Zvei rushed into the house, brought out the coat, and helped his son put it on. Just then Leah ran out the door and threw her arms around her son, sobbing hysterically. The larger soldier pried the mother from her son.

Israel was seized with anger and fear. He had grown up with Beryl Rosenbaum, his next-door neighbor, his boyhood friend and playmate. He wanted to do something, anything he could to help. But he and his father were powerless to intervene. They could only try to comfort Leah and Zvei.

As the soldiers dragged Beryl away to their waiting carriage, the mustachioed soldier suddenly turned and looked long and intensely at Israel. His penetrating gaze brought on a paralyzing grip of fear in the young man: the soldier seemed to be making a mental note about the presence of another conscript to meet his quota. Israel suddenly recalled what he had heard about what some men had done to avoid conscription. They had tried living on nothing but tea for months so they would be rail thin. Others, more desperate, cut off a finger. And he even heard of some who had blinded themselves. In that moment of terror, Israel felt as if an unseen force was taking hold of him and telling him he must somehow find a way to escape the uncertain fate that awaited his friend.

Chaim and Israel helped Zvei Rosenbaum get the sobbing Leah back into her home. As they approached the door they could hear the other six Rosenbaum children crying for their beloved brother. That day would forever be etched in Israel's memory.

The second influence on Israel came about on a trip to Warsaw with his Uncle Avrum. Boris Levinson had, as he often did, invited them into his home on a cold evening. He had also invited another guest named Lev Feinberg. A remarkable young businessman of thirty, Feinberg was in Warsaw as a buyer for an American company. He had emigrated to New York from Warsaw eight years earlier. The slender businessman had learned English through tireless effort and had diligently studied the ways of business and the customs of Americans from the first moment he arrived on America's shores. At the dinner table that evening he was peppered with questions about life in America by all three men, but mostly by the eager Israel.

Israel said, "They say the streets of America are paved with gold. Surely, that can't be true."

Lev, laughing, replied, "If there is such a street, I haven't found it. But in a way the gold is there. The gold is in the freedom and the possibility that anyone can succeed if he has enough ambition and works hard enough."

Boris requested, "Lev, tell them about democracy and freedom."

"Well, there are no kings and queens in America. The people choose their own leaders by voting for them. They are called legislators or congressmen or senators, and they make the laws. The governors and the president are elected by the people and the people can choose someone else if they don't like them."

Avrum asked, "How is it for Jews in America?"

Lev sighed and then explained, "First, you should know there are no pogroms and no conscriptions of our young men unless they are actually needed for a war. But while there is prejudice against Jews in many places, America is the best place for us that I know of. This is perhaps strange to you, but sadly I have discovered that there is some prejudice against us Jews from Poland and Russia by the German Jews who came to America many years ago."

Avrum probed further, "But can Jews live as Jews? You know, observe the Sabbath and Holy Days, eat kosher food, and follow our customs?"

Lev answered emphatically, "Yes, of course. In New York, where I live, there are many synagogues and rabbis. There are kosher markets and butcher shops. There are also Yiddish newspapers and theatres."

Israel chimed in, "What is New York like? Do you feel at home there? What about your family here in Warsaw?"

"Oh, I like New York very much, and I will soon feel very much at home, because you see, I have made arrangements to bring my father and mother, my grandfather, and my two sisters to America when I return to New York next month."

"But Lev," Israel said, "I have also heard stories about how crowded the Jewish area is in New York and how hard it is for newcomers to make a living. Are those stories true?"

"Israel," Lev said, "I'm glad you asked that question. There is a section in New York where most of the Jews have gathered. I lived there at first and although it was an exciting place, there was great poverty. There were just too many people living together in a small, very crowded, and sometimes dangerous place. I will be taking my family to another part of the city. I see you are asking many questions, Israel. Are you thinking about going to America?"

There was a long silence in the room and everyone looked expectantly at Israel, who was thinking hard about his answer to the question.

"Yes…yes," he declared. "I want to go to America and I would be interested in any advice you could give me."

Avrum was not entirely surprised by his nephew's declaration. They had spoken often about the idea. And now, as he looked at Israel and saw the eagerness in the young man's eyes, Avrum decided he would help make Israel's dream come true.

Responding to Israel, Lev said, "Yes, I do have some advice that I think would be good for you, or any young man who might be going to America. You know, America is a very large country with many big cities, some that are growing very fast. If I was just getting started I would not stay in New York. I might consider Boston, Philadelphia, Cleveland, Detroit, or Chicago."

Israel, who was getting very excited, replied, "I never heard of any of them but Chicago. Which one would you choose if you were going right now?"

"I would choose Cleveland. Let me tell you why. It is halfway between New York and Chicago. It is growing very rapidly. It has good business opportunities. And it has a lively Jewish community. Not only that, but I have a friend living there. He has a fur business. If you decide to go, I'll give you his name."

But it wasn't just that one meeting with Lev Feinberg or his fear of conscription that motivated Israel to fulfill his dream of emigrating to America. The third influence on Israel was that the Jews everywhere in Eastern Europe were aware that across the vast ocean there was that place of hope; a place where they would not be restricted to living in one particular area like the Pale of Settlement; a place where there wouldn't be the ever-present fear of pogroms, where the soldiers of the Czar, or even their gentile neighbors might suddenly swoop down and terrorize them in their homes and businesses; a place where they could find new modes and possibilities in their lives.

In between the time of the assassination of Czar Alexander II and the beginning of World War I, incredibly, as many as a third of the Eastern European Jews left their homelands in search of a better life. After a number of mostly young men had completed the journey, sending back flashes of hope, the numbers that followed became a flood of humanity.

Talk about America was surely discussed in Losice, as it was everywhere in large towns and small villages. The following is a quote from Irving Howe's book World of Our Fathers. It is attributed to a woman named Mary Antin who emigrated to America in 1891.

"America was in everybody's mouth. Businessmen talked about it over their accounts; the market women made up their quarrels that they might discuss it from stall to stall; people who had relatives in the famous land went around reading letters for the enlightenment of less fortunate folk…children played at emigrating; old folks shook their sage heads over the evening fire, and prophesied no good for those who braved the terrors of the sea and the foreign land beyond it; all talked of it, but scarcely anyone knew one true fact about this magic land."

And so, Israel was surrounded and engulfed with this new spirit; a kind of spirit that would inflame any ambitious young man who yearned for adventure and a chance to prove his worth.

Chapter 14

The Meeting with Chaim

Following their meeting with Boris Levinson and Lev Feinberg, on their return trip to Losice Israel and Avrum spoke of nothing but Israel's desire to go to America and what he would need to do to make the trip possible.

The first thing on Israel's mind was getting his father's blessing. Chaim Zynger had seen several other young men leave Losice to seek their fortune in America. But how he would react to Israel's plan was uncertain, at best. And then there was the deep love Israel felt for his mother, Dina, his two brothers, and his two baby sisters. He was already steeling himself for the terrible emotional scene he knew would be coming on the day of his departure, even though he wasn't certain it would all come to pass.

But he felt a degree of comfort in the most important part of his plan. He had seen firsthand situations where the sons of families had gone off to America and made enough money to bring their whole families to their new and better homes. He knew it would take a great deal of hard work and some good luck to be able to do such a thing but felt his chances of succeeding were as good as anyone else's.

When they reached Losice, Israel asked Avrum to help him talk to his father. Israel wanted to be sure the meeting was with his father alone. He knew his mother would be very emotional and might stop the meeting. Chaim was the head of his household, and as with other heads of families, his word was law. So, the meeting was held at Avrum's home, with only the three men.

"Father," Israel began, "there is something very important we want to talk to you about."

"Yes, so talk," Chaim replied. "I have sensed that something has been going on with you for some time."

"You remember that terrible day when the soldiers came and took Beryl away? I don't want to ever leave our family that way," Israel explained.

"Yes, I know that, my son. I have been worried about that for you and your brothers for a long time. The only way we could keep the soldiers away is by bribing them, but I'm afraid we don't have enough money to do that. So what is it that you are proposing to do?"

"Father, I want to go to America, and my Uncle Avrum is ready to help me."

"Avrum. Is this true?"

Avrum had been moving about the room, silently preparing glasses of tea as he listened to the conversation. He sat down at the table and looked intently at his brother-in-law.

"Yes, Chaim, not only is it true, but I believe it is a necessary and a wise thing."

"But it will take a great deal of money, and what about the papers?"

Avrum looked at Chaim and then at Israel, who was very encouraged by the way his father was reacting. Then he declared, "I will lend him the money for the trip. He can pay me back when he makes the money in America. I'll take care of getting him the necessary papers. I know some people who will help."

Chaim sat quietly, saying nothing for what felt like an eternity to Israel. He was thinking about the stories he had heard, of dozens of young men who had left their homes to take the long and hazardous journey, some dying along the way and others succeeding beyond their greatest hopes in America and then sending for the rest of their families. Finally, turning to his brother-in-law, he nodded his head slowly and spoke the words, "You would do this for my son? But why?"

"Chaim, you know that it is practically certain that he will face conscription in the army sooner or later. If and when that happens he may never return. You have seen what has happened to the sons of others in Losice. Israel is not only a hard worker. He is a strong and talented young man who deserves to have a better future than what his life will be here in Losice. I love Israel as if he were my own son and I want to help him realize his dream of going to America."

Chaim sat quietly while Israel held his breath. Chaim's thoughts then turned to his concern about whether his son would become lost as a Jew in that strange faraway country. With a deep sense of urgency, he broke his silence, asking, "Israel, will you be able to keep the Sabbath and observe the *Kashrut* (availability of kosher food) laws? Are there rabbis to guide you? What about synagogues?"

Avrum spoke first. "Yes, Chaim, there are thousands of Jews in America. Not only are there rabbis and synagogues and kosher food stores, but there are even Jewish organizations that help new settlers when they come to America."

Seeing that his argument was going well, Israel chimed in, "Father, I promise you I will never forget our ways. You have taught me well. I promise I will *daven* (pray) every day. You will always be proud of me."

Those words touched Chaim, who once again just sat quietly, thinking about what he would say next. He covered his eyes with both his hands and wept. The three men were silent. Then finally he spoke. "It will be hard for Dina and all of us, but I can see it will be the best thing for Israel. Son, you have my blessing."

When he heard those words, a chill ran through Israel's body. In that moment he recognized that life would never be the same again.

Chapter 15

Getting Ready

The next two months were spent preparing for the arduous trip. Israel prepared himself to be better able to cope with all the problems he expected, along the way and after his arrival in America. He sought out anyone who might know a little English, and any scraps of information he could gather from families that had relatives who had emigrated.

Israel had one more opportunity to meet with Lev Feinberg in Warsaw. Lev taught him many of the essential English words he would need and explained how American money worked. He also warned Israel about those who took advantage of young, inexperienced travelers, telling him to trust no one, especially if money was involved. And before they parted he gave Israel the name and address of his friend, the businessman Solomon Goldman in Cleveland.

In the meantime, Avrum had used his business connections to secure, with some well-placed bribes, a visa that would allow Israel to leave Poland and go through Germany and on to Antwerp, Belgium. There was a substantial difference in cost between second-class and steerage on the oceangoing vessels. Avrum pondered the alternatives over and over.

He thought, "If Israel goes by steerage he will have more money when he arrives and a better chance to establish himself. But if what I've heard about how bad steerage class is indeed true, Israel might get sick on the journey or be totally exhausted by the time he arrives in America. On the other hand, many have survived the trip, even the elderly. After all, Israel is young and strong." Finally, Avrum came to a decision: he would leave the choice up to Israel.

As the word that Israel was planning on going to America got around the community, there were varying responses from various people, some of whom admired him for daring the adventure, some who were jealous, and others who were perhaps a little too anxious to frighten him. One young man known as *Meshugenah Moyshe* (crazy Moses) took gleeful pleasure in inventing wild stories, just to see what kind of reaction he could evoke.

Moyshe, with unruly black curls surrounding his chubby face and a humorously evil twinkle in his slightly crossed brown eyes, came upon Israel one day in the street. He assailed Israel with a barrage of fabricated stories. "Israel, did you know that on the boat to America, if you get sick and they know you are a Jew they throw you into the sea?"

Israel replied, "No, Moyshe, I didn't know that. What other good news do you have for me today?"

"Israel, my friend," Moyshe declared, "you know my cousin Ruben, don't you? He told me that in America everybody has to eat *trafe* (non-kosher), like from dirty pigs and those things they call 'shrimp' or something like that."

"Is that so, Moyshe?" Laughing lustily, Israel retorted, "So all of a sudden you and your cousin Reuben who have never been further away than the village of Drohiczn are now experts on America."

And so it went with Mesugenah Moyshe: every time he could corner Israel, he fabricated greater fictions of calamities.

Israel also heard many stories of disasters that were true, like the tragedy that had befallen an unfortunate Losice family. The Zuckermans worked for years to scrape together the money to make the journey. They sold all their possessions except for the clothing they wore (with their money sewn into the linings of their coats), and their other possessions they carried in bundles and bags. They had lived through the horrors of traveling steerage class.

But when they arrived at Ellis Island their eleven-year-old daughter Rachel was found to have tuberculosis. She was to be sent back alone. The family couldn't allow that, so they all returned to Losice to start life anew in utter poverty. It was a cautionary tale about the importance of keeping healthy.

Israel knew a first-class ticket was not possible, and second-class would take most of the money from Avrum's loan. He thought, "If only I could find a few more rubles, I think I could get a second-class ticket and have enough money to get to Cleveland as well." Israel had saved up some money of his own, but it still wasn't enough.

It was now the night before he was to begin his journey and time to say good-bye to his father, mother, brothers, Hershel and Natan, and two baby sisters, Shayna and Sura Basha. The most emotional parting was with his mother, Dina. Dina asked Israel to make several promises, all the while knowing that he probably could not keep them all.

"Israel, my loved one, promise me you will write letters to us at least once every week."

"I will, Mama."

"Promise you will remember to put on your coat when it is cold so you won't get sick."

"I promise."

"Promise that in America you won't forget us."

"Mama, how could I forget you?"

"Israel, my son, look at me. If your father or I should die, promise you will say the *Kaddish* (memorial prayer) for us every Shabbat."

"Mama, don't talk that way!"

"Promise you will say a Kaddish."

"Yes, of course I will say a Kaddish, but that is a promise I don't expect to have to keep."

With that said, Dina reached down to a bag on the floor and pulled out twenty-four rubles. It was money she had been saving ever since she knew Israel would be leaving. She pressed the money into her son's hand. Israel rose up from his chair, came over to his mother, and held her close to him. They both wept the searing tears of loved ones who part not knowing if they will see one another ever again.

Chapter 16

The Adventure Begins

Avrum delivered Israel to the noisy, crowded train station in Warsaw. There were more people in this one place than Israel had ever seen in his entire young life.

Before he could board the train, Israel was directed to an office where officials were to inspect his papers. The inspector looked them over. Eyeing Israel suspiciously, he inquired, "Where are you going and why are you going there?"

Though nervous, Israel responded without hesitation, "I am going to Antwerp, Belgium, and from there to London to attend the wedding of my cousin."

The inspector said, "I see…." Then he took another more careful look at Israel's visa, which had actually been forged by a friend of Avrum.

The inspector was just about to get his magnifying glass out when there was a commotion in the line. A man was shouting, "This is an outrage! I want to talk to the magistrate." One of the other inspectors shouted, "Inspector Bronkowski, come here and help me with this trouble-maker!" Momentarily distracted, the inspector shook his head, picked up Israel's visa, and stamped it "Approved."

Relieved to have passed that first test, Israel had some time before the evening train was scheduled to leave. He walked about the station, taking in the sights.

Israel's clothing and his youthfully innocent manner was noticed by a man named Ignace Petrovski. Petrovski often loitered in the train station looking for ways to part travelers from their rubles. He stepped in front of Israel, startling him. A man of average height and weight, Ignace Petrovski sported a head of thick blond hair and, on his squarish face, a thick blond mustache to match it.

"Hello, comrade," he announced. "My name is Petrovski." Petrovski then bowed his head in a show of respect. "I can see you have never been here before. Oh, my young friend, I know this train station very well, and the many services that may be found nearby. Perhaps I can be of some assistance to you."

With that said, Petrovski locked his arm in Israel's, pulling him along, half talking, half whispering in a confidential way. "How would you like to go to a place where you will meet a very beautiful and very agreeable girl who will give you much pleasure for just a few rubles? You would like that, wouldn't you? You like redheads? How about blonds? I'll bet you have never been with a girl, have you? Come, tell the truth. We have the most beautiful girls in all of Poland here in Warsaw. You'll have such a good time. I can show you where the place is. Come this way....you'll see!"

Israel was taken aback for a few moments by this stranger Petrovski. He had never encountered anyone so aggressive. He remembered the advice he had been given about strangers who would try to take his money. The man's aggressiveness angered Israel, who was deceptively strong. He unlocked Petrovski's grip, pushing him away so hard he staggered and nearly fell.

"I don't know you," Israel shouted. "You are not my comrade or my friend. I don't want your help or your whores. Leave me alone!"

Surprised by the young man's fury but undaunted, Petrovski turned toward Israel and was about to again try to persuade him to go with him when he saw the fury in Israel's eyes. And when he noticed the young man's clenched fists, Petrovski gave up, turned, and disappeared into the hordes of humanity in the Warsaw train station.

Slightly shaken by the experience, Israel sat down on a bench to calm himself and wait for the eight o'clock train. A few minutes before the train arrived, an attractive blond teenage girl sat down at the far end of the bench. Though she was wearing a coat, it was apparent that she had a shapely figure. After a moment the girl looked over and smiled at Israel with a smile so charming that it momentarily left Israel breathless.

He had been slightly attracted to two pretty girls in Losice but had spoken few words to them—partially out of shyness and partially because he was so ambitious to explore and discover a different and better future, he had little time or interest in flirting with girls. But this girl, sitting on the bench....her smile, her pale blue eyes, her radiantly perfect skin, and something magical about the shape of her face altogether added up to something Israel had never encountered until that very instant. He thought, "She is the most beautiful girl I have ever seen. I hope she is getting on the train and I can find the courage to speak to her."

Israel was thinking hard about what he could say to the beautiful girl. He thought, "I'll ask her where she is from and maybe where she is going." He looked over at her and smiled. She smiled in return. He continued to gather his courage and was just about to ask his question when the train arrived and an older woman came up to the girl and, speaking in Yiddish, said, "Come, Nadja. We must find some good seats."

The woman glanced at Israel with a look of disapproval. As they headed for the train, the girl turned her head toward Israel and smiled once again.

Chapter 17

Nadja

Israel followed Nadja and the woman he believed was either her mother or her aunt as they boarded the train. As people crowded onto the train, Israel lost sight of the girl. After trying to find her for several minutes without success he decided to find a seat and look for her as soon as he could. This was to be his first train ride and he knew it would be a very long one—twenty-five hours or more!

His mind was overflowing with excitement at the thought of what lay ahead: moving at a speed he had never experienced before; seeing a part of Poland he had never seen before, and then Germany and Belgium; actually taking meals on the train; meeting other travelers; finding his way by boat to England; and the long and dangerous crossing of the great ocean to a new world and a new life. And though he thought of all those things, one idea dominated all of them: that beautiful girl who had smiled at him.

It had been a very long day. It was dark now and little could be seen through the window. Though he struggled to stay awake so he could look for the girl again, Israel succumbed to the hypnotic drone of the rolling train. He dozed off for an hour. Waking with a start, he decided to take a walk through the train, with the hope that he would find the elusive girl. He thought, "Was she real or did I imagine her? She was so beautiful. I don't see how she could be anything other than a dream. But if she is real, how will I be able to meet her? That woman with her didn't like me, I could see that."

Israel, walking through the train, had reached the third car. He was about to continue on to the fourth one when the door of the women's restroom opened and out came the dream girl. They stopped and looked at one another, not moving for several seconds. Suddenly, Israel began to talk and words flowed from him in a volume he had never experienced before.

"Hello. My name is Israel Zynger. I am traveling from my home in Losice. Do you know where that is? It's a small town about ninety kilometers from Warsaw. I am a leather-worker. I have been working for my Uncle Avrum in his shoe factory. My father is a great sofer. He writes beautiful and perfect Torahs. I have two brothers and two baby sisters. My mother, Dina, is a great woman. She keeps a wonderful home for all of us and also trades many different goods at the markets. I am taking the train all the way to Antwerp on my way to America."

The girl didn't say anything. She just stood still for a while, absorbing all she had heard. Finally she spoke.

"Hello, Israel Zynger. My name is Nadja Birnbaum. I am traveling from my home in Lodz with my Aunt Ludmila. My father works at the I.K. Poznanski plant in Lodz. We are on a trip to visit my uncle's family in a town near Cologne. That is in Germany. You are very brave to be traveling to America...."

Suddenly Nadja stopped, putting her hand over her mouth. She then said, "I shouldn't be talking to you. It isn't proper, you know. My aunt will be very angry with me if she finds out."

"Where is your aunt now?"

"She is in the next car, sleeping."

Desperate to hold on to his fragile connection with Nadja, Israel said, "This will be a very long trip. Do you think there might be other times when we could talk? I don't want to make trouble for you with your aunt, but I would love to learn more about you."

Nadja's Aunt Lumila was, fortunately for the two young people, a deep sleeper. Over the next several hours Israel and Nadja managed to find many stolen moments. When they were together they shared not only the story of their own lives but also all about the lives of their family members. And as time passed they expressed their deeper feelings about life and their hopes for the future. Israel experienced a delicious torture sitting or sometimes standing near Nadja and knowing he dare not think about touching her. After each of the four times they met he could think of nothing but the next time he would see her.

The train had stopped in Berlin, where many passengers got off and new ones took their seats. Israel dreaded the thought that the next major stop would be Cologne. There was a desperation in his conversations with Nadja that grew as the train neared the city of Cologne and its great cathedral. As they pulled into the station, Israel wondered if he would have a chance to say good-bye to Nadja. He had heard about a thing called falling in love, but didn't really understand what that meant. He thought, "Is this what they call falling in love? It is wonderful, beautiful, and very frightening. I think I am in love with Nadja, but I don't know how she feels about me. But what does it matter? She will be getting off the train soon and I'll probably never see her again."

During the last hours, as the train neared Cologne, Israel and Nadja couldn't manage to see one another. Israel sat near the window, desperately hoping he would catch a glimpse of Nadja when she left the train.

But Nadja and her Aunt Ludmila had just gotten off the train from an exit two cars back from where Israel was seated. As soon as they reached the platform, Nadja turned to her aunt and announced, "I left something on the train. I will be right back." Her aunt responded, "I'll come with you." Nadja waved her off, saying, "I won't need any help. Don't worry. I'll be right back."

Before her aunt could do or say anything, Nadja worked her way onto the train through a crowd of people. She rushed through the passageway until she found Israel, sitting in his seat with a forlorn look on his face, staring out the window.

She tapped his shoulder. He stood. Nadja kissed Israel full on the mouth.

Then she was gone. It was a kiss he would remember for a lifetime.

Chapter 18

Antwerp

Israel's sadness at seeing Nadja leave was great, but he didn't let it overcome him. Moment by moment there were new experiences and challenges to keep his mind occupied. With Nadja gone he began to talk to some of the other passengers whom he heard speaking Yiddish or Polish. The day was sunny and that picked up his spirits. He marveled at the blazing quality of the light as he gazed at the fields and forests, the ancient towns and the ruins of old castles along the way. He also spent every moment he could studying a book of English language phrases. He prepared himself to express the words he might need in French to find his way to the ferry to England.

By the time the train was nearing Antwerp Israel had become acquainted with three other passengers. One, a kindly old German man with a remarkably pleasant disposition, appeared to be very knowledgeable about everything. Speaking to that man with a combination of Polish, Yiddish, and the few words in German he could remember, Israel asked, "What language do they speak in Antwerp?"

The man responded, "Flemish and French. I don't know any Flemish, but I can speak some French. Are there some words that might help you when you get there?"

"Yes, how do I ask about the boat to England?"

At first the man didn't quite understand the question, because of Israel's strange combination of languages. The man went over the words to himself for a minute or two until he suddenly smiled, looked up, and said, "I understand. It's about the boat to England. Isn't it?

The old man continued, "I believe you would ask *Ou est le bateau pour l' Angleterre?*"

Israel said, "Thank you. Can you please say that again?" The man repeated it. Then Israel repeated the words several more times.

It was late morning when the train arrived in gloomy, overcast Antwerp. Israel picked up his suitcase and said good-bye to the old man and the other two passengers he had befriended on the train. He set out on the streets of the strange city to look for the boat to England.

At first he walked about aimlessly, taking in the sights of the city: the architecture of the quaint buildings, the way the people looked and how they were dressed, the signs on the street and on the stores. It was a culture very different from what he had always known. But when a light rain chilled the air, he looked for someone who could help him find his way. He came upon two young men about his age and began to ask the taller of the two his question.

"*Oues...le... bat....bat...por...por... Angle, Angle....te....te...ter?*" That was the best he could do to remember the words.

The young men looked at one another and laughed. The shorter man mockingly repeated, "*Oues le bat bat pour pour Angle Angle te te ter?*"

They both looked at Israel, threw up their hands, indicating they didn't understand him, and turned and walked away.

Israel, unfazed by what had happened, stopped and asked an old woman as she came out of her house. His question was overheard by a man delivering milk to the house next door. The milkman and the woman discussed what they thought the strange young man had attempted to ask. Then the milkman said, "*Bateau pour l' Angleterre.*"

When the woman agreed that was possibly what the man wanted to know, they both started talking at once in French, trying explain where he could get the boat to England. The problem was, they didn't agree on the best route. Soon they were arguing and shouting at one another. They became so agitated and involved in their argument, they stopped paying attention to Israel altogether. He stood listening to what sounded like rapid-fire gibberish as the argument heated up.

The old woman shouted "*Tu es un imbécile!*" (You're a complete moron!) As a retort the milkman yelled, "*Ot'a bercé trop pres du mur?*" (As a child, was your cradle rocked too close to the wall?) Shaking his head in confusion and disbelief, Israel turned and walked away in what he thought might be the direction the milkman had intended to send him.

The sky had darkened and a steady light rain had begun. Israel, carrying his suitcase, walked down Stadionstraat to Atletenstraat. He took shelter in the doorway of what appeared to be an official public building. There was no one on the street.

Israel had never felt so alone in his life. The gloom engulfed him as he assessed his situation. He was alone, hundreds of kilometers from home, in a foreign city where people spoke a puzzling language and acted strangely—certainly not at all friendly. It was cold and dark and depressingly gloomy. Thunder roared, as if to mock him as all these thoughts and feelings swept over him. A flash of lightning signaled a heavier cascade of rain. As if all that wasn't enough to bear, Israel's stomach growled and he remembered he hadn't eaten for several hours.

At that moment he had a spark of a memory about something that might help him. Israel thought, "Now what was it I had heard about that was in Antwerp? Avrum's friend Levinson in Warsaw said something about it." Israel tried to reconstruct that conversation of some two years earlier.

"Yes," he thought. "That's it! He wrote something on a piece of paper and gave it to me. Let me see. I think I may have it." Israel, now a bit more hopeful, looked through his pockets, but the paper was not there. He looked into one of his bags. Reaching down to the bottom, he felt something. There it was.

It only had two words written on it and he wasn't sure what they meant. But he was certain that they were supposed to help him if he had a problem in Antwerp.

A distinguished-looking white-haired man came out of the building. Using hand motions to get his attention, Israel stepped in front of the man and read what it said on the scrap of paper: "Hollandse...Bouwmeesterstraat?"

The man looked at Israel and guessed from his appearance and clothing that he was looking at a young Jewish immigrant. The man nodded his understanding, repeated the name "Bouwmeesterstraat," and motioned Israel to follow him as he opened a large black umbrella. Israel followed and the man offered to share the umbrella. They briskly walked three blocks together through the downpour.

They turned a corner and the man pointed to a tall, majestic building with a Star of David adorning the huge doorway. The man pointed to the door. Israel tried the handle. At first the door wouldn't budge. The man encouraged him with a hand motion and a nod. Israel tried again, and the door opened.

As the kind man waved good-bye, Israel turned to him and, not remembering what to say in French, instead said "Shalom." He entered the Historic Hollandse Synagogue, not sure why the man had led him there, but with hope in his heart that he would find the help he needed.

Chapter 19

In the Synagogue

Closing the door behind him and happy to be out of the rain, Israel looked wide-eyed at the huge interior of the ornate synagogue, which was not only the largest one he had ever seen, but was also the newest. At first it was very quiet. Then he heard someone speaking at the far end of the mostly dark large space. It sounded like it was coming from where the *bimah* (elevated platform used by the rabbi and cantor) would be. "Yes," he thought. "They must be getting ready for the *Maariv* (evening prayer) service."

With that thought, Israel moved automatically into ritual mode. Looking around, he saw a rack covered with *talesim* (prayer shawls), selected one, said the prayer for donning it, and put it over his shoulders. Then he walked to the front of the synagogue.

When he came into view, a short man with a long gray beard in rabbinical attire smiled broadly and declared in Yiddish to the eight men sitting in the first two rows of pews, "We have a minyan. Let us begin."

Without asking his name, the rabbi handed Israel a *Machzor* (prayer book). The men all stood up and began chanting, "*Shema Yisarel Adonai Elohenu Adonai Echad!*" (Hear, oh Israel, the Lord our God, the Lord is one!) While some of the inflections were slightly different, Israel felt his spirit lifted by the experience of reciting those familiar words and joining a group of praying men, just as he had done hundreds of times before. His spirit was lifted even more because he had heard the rabbi speaking Yiddish and knew he would now be able to make himself understood.

It was obvious to the rabbi that the young stranger was no stranger to *davening* (traditional chanting, praying while moving the body slightly). When the brief service concluded, the rabbi greeted Israel, asking his name and where he was from. Just as he had done on the train when he met Nadja the day before, Israel found himself bursting with the need to tell who he was and what he was doing in Yiddish.

"Thank you, Rabbi. My name is Israel Zynger. I am traveling from my home in Losice, Poland. My father, Chaim Zynger, is a well-known sofer." When he said that, the rabbi and most of the men nodded in approval. Israel continued, "I am on my way to America. I have been trying to find where to go to find the boat to London, where my father's brother lives. But I got lost.

A kind man showed me to this beautiful synagogue."

A tall, well-dressed man named Jumi Hoffman, who was wearing a ring with an enormous diamond, said to Israel, "I can show you how to get to the boat tomorrow, but where are you staying tonight?"

Israel answered, "I don't know. I had hoped to be on the boat to England."

The rabbi spoke up, saying, "Can one of you help this young man tonight? After all, he helped us. Without him would not have a minyan."

The men all nodded in agreement. Hoffman, who was a prosperous diamond merchant, took charge, saying, "Come along, young man. My family would enjoy the opportunity to do the *mitzvah* (good deed) of helping a fellow Jew, the son of a sofer. And, tell me, have you eaten your dinner?"

Israel, overcome with joy at his good luck, answered, "Sir, you are very kind. How can I ever thank you? No, I haven't had anything to eat for several hours."

"Well then," Hoffman said, "come along and you will find out what fine food we have here in Antwerp."

Chapter 20

On to London

The evening at the home of his host proved delightful in every respect. When they entered Mr. Hoffman's large and comfortable home, a short distance from the synagogue, Israel was overwhelmed with a plethora of sensations. The home was far better furnished than any other he had ever seen. A magnificent six-foot-tall wood-encased grandfather clock stood in the hallway, its Roman numerals encrusted with diamonds. Israel stood staring at it until Mr. Hoffman urged him on into the parlor.

The floors were covered with ornate, hand-woven Oriental rugs, and the room was furnished with overstuffed chairs and a huge sofa. Heavy, richly colored curtains hung at all the windows. There were more bookcases than he had ever seen in a private home, and cabinets filled with hand-blown decorative glass and vases filled with red and yellow tulips. The dining room table was covered with an exquisite white linen tablecloth and set with fine bone china and gleaming sterling silver flatware.

Israel looked around in amazement at the lamps, which provided more light than he had ever seen. Rather than candles or common kerosene lamps, the room was lit with "Aladdin" lamps. Though they burned kerosene, each was equivalent to a 100 watt bulb.

After gawking at the splendor of the home, the delicious odors of cooking and baking emanating from the kitchen that were tantalizing to Israel, especially since he was so very hungry.

Israel was invited to sit down to dinner with the very large Hoffman family, which included eight children, ages one to eighteen. After the delicious dinner of traditional Belgian food—steak marinated in beer and various vegetable dishes, followed by Belgian waffles—Mr. Hoffman related some of the history of the Jewish diamond cutters of Antwerp.

He said, "Antwerp has for hundreds of years been a very important European seaport. Diamonds flowed through the city after their discovery in South Africa in the 1860s. That brought many Jewish diamond cutters. Along with the cutters, there are jewelry designers and craftsmen and, of course, merchants like me."

Hoffman's children were curious about their unexpected guest and peppered him with questions.

"Tell us what your house looks like."

"Do you have any brothers or sisters?"

"Tell us about your train ride. It must have been very exciting."

"What will you do in America?"

Then one of the girls said, "You are so brave to go to America all alone. I can't imagine what that would be like."

Israel answered all of their questions as well as he could; the conversation became very animated. But later, as he lay in bed exhausted from his long adventure-filled day, he was overcome with a great surge of homesickness as he tried to fall asleep in the beautiful but strange house.

He was awakened early the next morning and guided to the ferry terminal by Jacob, the oldest Hoffman son. Stepping onto the ferry was exhilarating for Israel. It was the largest ship he had ever seen and it was heading out on the largest body of water he had ever seen: the North Sea.

He tried to recognize what was being said by the other passengers, some speaking in French, some Flemish, and some English. He guessed that they were saying that the sea was unusually calm that day. Israel couldn't stop looking at the sea as it rolled by for several hours until land was sighted: England. After landing at Dover, Israel found his way to the carriage that would take him to the great city of London and the home of his uncle, Jacob Usher Zynger.

Chapter 21

Looking for the Zyngers of London

When Israel first saw Warsaw, he had been overwhelmed by the size of the city, the hordes of people, and all the impressive buildings, but when he arrived in London he began to think of Warsaw in a different way. As he approached London, one of the greatest historic cities of the world, Israel took in the incredible sights as his carriage passed cathedrals, palaces, the Houses of Parliament and homes of splendor far beyond his experience.

Finally the carriage arrived at the station in the city, where the passengers got off and dispersed in all directions to their various destinations. Israel looked about for help and noticed a uniformed man standing behind an imposing counter. After studying his notes, he asked the man, "Can tell how go Carter Street?"

The man looked over the young foreign traveler. It was obvious from the clothing he wore that the young man was from somewhere in Eastern Europe. Israel wore a simple wool cap, a loose-fitting jacket, and boots that covered the lower part of his trousers. Saying nothing, the man behind the counter dipped his pen into an inkwell and wrote these words on a small piece of scrap paper: "Whitechapel High Street" to "Houndsditch" to "Carter Street." Handing Israel the paper, the man smiled warmly and motioned toward the street they were situated on, saying "Whitechapel High Street." Then he pointed to the left and sent Israel on his way.

Israel thanked the man, picked up his bag, and walked briskly down Whitechapel High Street. It was near sunset on what had been an unusually beautiful day. Israel pushed himself to walk as fast as possible, to avoid having to travel in the large, noisy, crowded, and confusing city in the approaching darkness.

After walking several blocks he saw a sign he guessed read "Houndsditch," but he didn't want to take the chance that he was wrong. After the unpleasant experience he'd had in Antwerp he was cautious about who to ask for help.

He stood at the intersection for several minutes, resting until he noticed a police officer coming his way. His first instinct was to avoid the policeman if he could. Past experiences of his family and friends had showed that men in uniforms, whether soldiers or policemen, were seldom pleasant, and could often be dangerous if you had no money to offer a bribe. But this short, stout policeman was at that moment joking with an older woman and looked completely harmless, even in his well-starched uniform.

Israel waited until the banter between the two had ended. He stepped up to the policeman and pointing to the street sign, asking slowly and carefully, "Hounds-itch?"

The officer laughed at the mispronunciation and then nodded, saying, "I believe you are referring to the beautiful street with the dignified name, Houndsditch. Yes, that is certainly the name of this street." With that said he turned, swung his nightstick over his shoulder, and whistled a tune as he strolled down the street.

Israel hurried down Houndsditch, not entirely certain why the policeman had laughed so heartily. It was nearly nighttime and he wanted to find his uncle's home as soon as possible. He was looking for the Polish synagogue on Carter Street. He had been told to find that building first and then ask people in the neighborhood where to find the Zynger family.

As he reached the next intersection he peered down the new street in the fading light. What he saw warmed his heart. It was a sign in large Yiddish letters advertising a kosher butcher shop—and there were other signs as well: a bakery, a delicatessen, and several others. He strode down the street filled with anticipation.

But as he continued to walk he suddenly felt confusion. He could see that the street came to an abrupt end in about two hundred feet.

Israel was overcome by a feeling of dread. He was alone in the huge city and didn't know where he would be able to spend the night. Noticing another street branching off Carter, he walked down that street, and still saw no building that looked anything like any synagogue he had ever seen before. There were many people on the street, all of whom seemed to be in a great hurry. Israel stopped momentarily and looked around, when a woman in her thirties, accompanied by a young girl with flaming-red hair, stopped in front of Israel.

Speaking in a clear and precise Yiddish, the woman said, "Young man, you look a bit lost. Can I help you?"

Israel looked at the woman and the girl, who was obviously her daughter, and responded in his Polish-accented Yiddish, "Can you tell me where I can find the Polish synagogue? I didn't see anything that looked like a synagogue anywhere on these streets."

The attractive middle-age woman nodded knowingly, motioning to Israel to follow her as she strode down the short street. They passed in front of an office building. Just as they reached the far end of the building she turned to the lost young Israel and said, "The Polish synagogue is in this building, but there wouldn't be anyone in at this hour."

Dismayed, Israel thanked the woman for trying to help him and then said, "I don't know what I can do now. I was told that someone at the synagogue would be able to tell me how to find my Uncle Jacob Usher Zynger's house."

The woman looked at her daughter and both of them looked at Israel and started laughing. "So you are the nephew Jacob has been telling us about," the woman said. "Come, we were on our way to visit our dear friends, the Singer family. Oh, by the way, they changed their name from Zynger to Singer."

The smile on Israel's face could have lit up the entire neighborhood. In a few short moments he had gone from gloom and despair to total elation. Now he was being accompanied down the street by a remarkably attractive woman wearing a heavenly fragrance, along with her strikingly pretty redheaded daughter.

The Singers lived in the last house on the short street. It was a townhouse typical of the neighborhood: brick and stone, with large windows facing the street. The sidewalk came right up to their door and there were no trees or grass to be seen. An impressive brass door-knocker was mounted on the big black door. When Israel noticed the ornate *Mezuzah* (a piece of parchment in a decorative case with specific prayers from the Torah) on the doorpost, he touched it and kissed his fingers, as is the custom when entering a Jewish home.

When the door opened, a large black-bearded man wearing a yarmulke greeted the woman and her daughter, declaring, "Welcome Mrs. Greenbaum, and who is the young man with you?"

"Jacob, it's your nephew from Poland. We found him wandering around the street."

Seeing his nephew, the oldest son of his brother Chaim, for the first time in many years, Jacob turned his head back inside the house and shouted, "Come, come everyone. Israel is here on his way to America..." He paused and, turning to Israel, asked, "That is your name, isn't it?" When Israel nodded, Jacob again shouted, saying, "Let's give him a proper Singer family welcome."

In a few seconds the hallway was filled with the Singer family members: Mrs. Jane Olga Singer and their three sons, Barney, Joe, and Mokey. Israel was pulled into the swarm of bodies and first kissed on the cheek by his uncle, then by Mrs. Singer, and then by the three boys. Jacob declared to Israel, "We are a kissing family. I hope you don't mind."

Israel blushed. The redness in his cheeks deepened when Mrs. Greenbaum, not wanting to miss out on the fun, kissed Israel and then motioned for her daughter to do so as well. The girl with the flaming red hair looked up at Israel and said, "My name is Dorothy, and one day I too will go to America." With that she planted another kiss on Israel's cheek.

Later that evening, as he lay in bed thinking about all he had experienced that day, for a reason he could neither understand nor explain, the one thought that filled his mind was his encounter with young Dorothy Greenbaum.

Israel stayed in the welcoming arms of the Singer family for two weeks. During that time his uncle showed him around the great city. He also spent a lot of his time telling the family what life was like in Losice and about his family, whom they had never met. Mrs. Greenbaum and her daughter visited frequently and Dorothy continued to demonstrate her strong to desire to go to America, once even declaring, "Oh, Israel, won't you take me with you?"

Dorothy made it her special mission to teach Israel as much English as she could during the time he was in London, while cautioning him that the Americans spoke a peculiar kind of English that he might find difficult to understand. Israel found the young girl to be, though only twelve, very grown up in so many ways. He pictured how she would look in a few years. By the time he was ready to leave he made a secret pledge to himself: he would marry that girl someday!

Chapter 22

On the *Carmania*

With the help of his uncle, Israel booked passage on the *Carmania*, a ship that was launched in 1905 and carried 2,600 passengers from Liverpool to New York. Because the ship was so new, passage on it was expensive.

Israel wanted to sail on the ship, but felt the only way he could afford the trip was in steerage. Though he had heard horror stories about steerage, he reasoned that if the situation got unbearable he might be able to upgrade part of the trip, thereby at least saving some of his money.

The day was blustery cold with intermittent snow showers when Israel prepared to climb aboard the vessel. As he approached the dock he gazed in awe at the huge smokestacks towering over the deck of the ship.

Soon he found himself jostled by the ever-increasing crowd. What a dizzying scene! Hundreds of passengers—men, women, and children of all ages—formed a crush of humanity. Everyone seemed, like him, excited and apprehensive about the journey; many tightly clutched boxes, suitcases, and bags as if they were talismans that would protect them from the dangers that lay ahead. Mothers nursed infants. Small children wailed pitifully. Fathers shouted at errant teenagers, imploring them to stay close.

The Italians would bring to America pasta, pizza, and the operas of Giuseppe Verdi. A few of the Sicilians brought the Cosa Nostra to New York and other big cities ripe for takeovers by the Mob. The Irish were heading to Boston, where their ancestors settled after fleeing the great Potato Famine. They would supply the city with policemen and priests, laborers and housemaids. The Eastern European Jews would peddle their wares; some would end up owning department stores while others wrote America's songs and became the darlings of Broadway and Hollywood. There were Germans, Greeks, Hungarians, Czechs, Romanians, Poles, and Russians. Israel heard many languages on the ship and picked up quite a few words that would help him along the way.

Before they had reached this beginning point in their journey, Israel and all the others had passed through an obstacle course of requirements set by the governments of the passengers and the steamship line. Doctors examined everyone, because if they arrived at Ellis Island and failed to pass the physical exam they would be sent back to Europe at the ship's expense. The steamship line officials walked about shouting as they herded the crowd on board and into their ticketed areas. The crew prepared to get the ship underway.

When he showed his ticket, Israel was directed to the steerage area down in the bowels of the ship, where the stirring screws never ceased their unpleasant grinding. He claimed the middle of the three filthy bunks. The area was overcrowded, foul-smelling, and noisy. He knew he couldn't stand being in that dank, dirty place any more than he absolutely had to. He intended to escape the steerage area for as long as possible. After stowing his bags he climbed the slippery, steep narrow stairs, determined to explore the ship from bow to stern. Unable to understand the signs that said "Keep Out" or "Crew Members Only," he explored many places forbidden to passengers until crew members ejected him.

After an hour of exploration, Israel became hungry and inquired about where the food was being served by using pantomimed gestures of eating.

Now he faced a dilemma. The food on the ship was not kosher. He saw that some of the Jews had prepared themselves by bringing along some of their own food—but he hadn't. He was hungry and knew he couldn't survive on water alone for the entire journey. Rationalizing that he would need all his strength when he arrived in America, he felt his parents and possibly even God would forgive him. He stood in line, first to get the dinner pail provided by the steamship company, and then in the second line, where the thin stew was served from huge kettles.

That night and every night of the journey Israel and the other unfortunates tried to sleep in that place of filth and stench and constant seasickness, breathing air whose oxygen had been replaced by foul gases.

Israel had always been in good health except for one ailment that was ubiquitous in his family from time to time during certain seasons of the year: allergies, probably to spring grasses, led to asthmatic attacks. But now, for the first time, Israel began to suffer asthma attacks brought on by dust and foul air. His only relief came by climbing the steps to the main deck of the ship, where the sea air cleared his lungs. But the asthma brought with it a great concern that weighed on him heavily. Would he be well enough when the ship arrived in America? Would he pass the examination?

As one self-educated immigrant who experienced steerage at that time reported:

> "On board we became utterly dejected. We were all herded together in a dark, filthy compartment in steerage.... Seasickness broke out among us. Hundreds of people had vomiting fits.... As all were crossing the ocean for the first time, they thought their end had come. The confusion of cries became unbearable...I wanted to escape from

that inferno but no sooner had I thrust my head forward from the lower bunk than someone from above me vomited straight on my head. I wiped the vomit away, dragged myself onto the deck, leaned against the railing, and vomited my share into the sea, and lay down half-dead upon the deck."[4]

The environment Israel found himself in was far more challenging than any he had ever encountered. There were hostile, pushy passengers, ill-mannered and noisy. Early on he learned how to keep the bullies from pushing ahead in the food line. Once he witnessed a young man trying to steal a coat from a frail, aged rabbi. Israel intervened. When confronted by Israel, the thief drew a knife from his pocket. Israel didn't hesitate. He produced his gleaming leather cutting tool and threw his arm out in a slashing movement, scaring the thief as he shouted, "How much of your blood is that old rabbi's coat worth to you?"

The frightened would-be thief laid the coat down and flew from the area. Israel experienced that and more as the *Carmania* made its way across the wide ocean. He underwent powerful changes, changes that toughened him, steeled his spine, and prepared him for the trials to come.

The most terrifying times were the days and nights when the ship was sailing blindly through dense fog. The mournful sound of the foghorn chilled the bones and warned of the danger of collision with other blinded ships and hidden icebergs. There were the sleepless days and nights of storms, when the ship groaned as it was tossed about by towering seas.

From the ninth day on, Israel stood for long hours on the deck looking toward the West, hoping to get his first glance of the new world. Then on the eleventh day he heard someone shout, "There she is—the lady with the lamp!" Soon the deck of the ship was crowded. As they drew closer to the 300-foot-tall Statue of Liberty gleaming in the morning sun, the immigrants suddenly became quiet as they gazed at the symbol of freedom and hope. Every man, woman, and child in that moment was dreaming of what their life could be in this new and strange land.

While the people were relieved that their miserable journey would soon end, many were filled with anxiety. Would they and every member of their family pass the examinations? What questions would they have to answer, and would they know what to say? Where would they spend the first night? How would they ever be able to learn that impossible language?

And the worst question: God forbid—would they be sent back?

---

[4] Quotation from *World of Our Fathers,* by Irving Howe

Chapter 23

Ellis Island

Recalling that life-changing experience many years later, Israel told his Ellis Island story to his two older daughters, Lillian and Shirley:

> When I first came to America on the boat, we were going to land at a place called Ellis Island near New York City. An announcement was made in lots of different languages, for everyone to gather their things and come out on the deck. Then they put us in special groups according to the ship's manifest.
>
> We were herded onto a place they called the Customs Wharf and pushed along. Oy, what a tumult! They were yelling at us to get moving in half a dozen languages. When we reached Ellis Island we were all put into a great big room in a building, and they separated us into a lot of different lines.
>
> We first had to see the doctor. Everyone was nervous, and so was I because I could see what was happening at the front of some of the lines. Most people were examined and then passed on to another line. But some of the poor people had their coats marked with colored chalk. They were put into a caged place, apart from the rest of us. I will never forget the looks on their faces. I found out that the doctors thought those people might have weak hearts, or hernias, or things like that—or maybe that they might be *meshuga* (crazy).
>
> When I got to the front of the line the doctor listened to my chest. I was very worried that he would hear some sounds from my asthma. He listened for a long time. Then he called over another doctor to listen. 'Oy vey!' I thought. 'They're going to send me back!' The second doctor said something to the first doctor, in English. I couldn't understand what they were saying. Then the first doctor told me to go to the next line with all the people who passed the first test. I was so relieved! My asthma was gone. I guess it was because of the

fresh sea air.

The next doctor was looking for diseases like tuberculosis and the ones you could get from…well, I can't tell you about that until you're older. Then there was a doctor who lifted up our eyelids in a painful way. He made the children cry. I don't know why they do that!

Thank God! I was through with the doctors, but then there was the inspector, who would be asking many questions. As I waited in line I must have looked very nervous, because truthfully after seeing what had happened to some of the others I was terrified that I might say the wrong thing. Then I could be in big trouble. So there I was, thinking to myself 'I am a tough guy' but shaking. A man wearing a uniform with a hat that had some letters on it came over and spoke to me in English. He asked, 'What is your name, young man, and where are you coming from?' When I told him in Yiddish that I didn't understand him, I was surprised: he repeated his questions in a very haimish Yiddish. After I answered him he told me, 'I'm from the Hebrew Immigrant Aid Society*[5] and I'm here to help Jewish immigrants.' He told me to stop worrying and that everything would be okay. Then he gave me advice about the best way to answer the questions the inspector would be asking me. Having his help calmed me down. Then he gave me the address of the Society and said, 'If you ever need any help come to our office.' He was the first person in America to offer me a helping hand. I will never forget his kindness.

Finally, I came to the inspector. I didn't understand all his questions. I never heard of anarchism or polygamy. He asked me if I had a job waiting. I told him, 'No, but I have skills as a shoemaker and furrier.' He wanted to know things like who paid my passage, had I ever been in prison, and if I could read and write. My answers must have been the right ones. When he looked my papers over he said, 'Your name is Israel Zynger? In America you should make your last name Singer, S-I-N-G-E-R. That will be more American.' I agreed. He wrote down my new name, stamped my papers, smiled at me, and pointed

---

[5] The Hebrew Immigrant Aid Society was formed in New York City in 1892. It came about because of the huge numbers of Jews who were arriving at Ellis Island every day needing help of all kinds. The HIAS representatives often acted as advocates for the immigrants by restraining authorities, who were too often inclined to turn away new arrivals for unjust reasons. The HIAS, though formed specifically to help Jews, often helped Christians as well, since there wasn't anyone else to help them through the rigors of Ellis Island.

the way to the ferry boat to New York City.

Lillian and Shirley loved hearing that story and asked their father to repeat it many times.

Chapter 24

Manhattan

Before boarding the ferry, Israel was directed to a window, where he was told he could exchange his rubles for American money. The clerk counted out forty-seven dollars and sixty-three cents. That was all Israel would have to sustain him until he could find work. And he was better off than many of the immigrants. He had enough to rent a room for two or three months. A three-room apartment could be rented for about $10 a month. Typical food prices at the time were: one pound of fish, eight cents, six eggs, thirteen cents, three pounds of oatmeal, ten cents, one pound of coffee, fifteen cents.

Israel boarded the ferry to Manhattan. As he neared the fabled city he felt as if his heart would burst with exhilaration. At that moment he had no fear or apprehension about what might lay ahead—only the confidence and optimism of a young man embarking on a great adventure.

When the ferry reached the dock, the immigrants poured out and headed in all directions. Some had relatives or friends waiting. There were emotional, tearful scenes as families were reunited with the men who had struggled, in many cases for years, to gather enough money to bring their families to America.

While there were a few government agents to assist the new arrivals, the area was also plagued with con men offering their services in order to fleece the last few dollars from their immigrant victims. Israel looked like fruit ripe for the picking. He was young and traveling alone. A swarthy, well-dressed man with a waxy mustache approached Israel and asked him in Italian-accented English, "Where you a-going young man? Perhaps—" but before he could go on, another man, taller and heavier wearing a shabby fur-collar coat, interrupted, saying, "Luigi, can't you see he is one of ours? He won't understand you."

With that, the man deftly came between Israel and the Italian, and declared in Yiddish, "Perchik Rosenberg at your service. You are very fortunate I came to your rescue. That goy doesn't know anything. I know New York better than anybody else. For fifty cents, I will tell you how to find whatever you want. You want to take the elevated car? Wait till you see that. It's up in the air. You won't believe it when you see it. How about the subway? Oy! It flies underground like a tornado. You're going to the Bronx? How about Brooklyn? You got relatives? Tell me about them. Are you from Poland? I'll bet we're related. You have relatives named Rosenberg? Maybe we're cousins. What do you think? Show me your money and I'll tell how much is fifty cents."

He was a fast talker. His chatter had a dizzying effect on Israel. But when Perchik asked to see his money, Israel's mind cleared. He remembered the man who had approached him in the Warsaw train station and the warnings about those he might encounter on his trip who would try to take his money.

"Thank you, Mr. Perchik, or whatever your name is. I don't need your help. Good-bye!"

Not easily discouraged, Rosenberg grabbed Israel's arm as he turned to leave and declared, "Come on, cousin. I can show you the wonders of Manhattan you could never imagine."

Israel stopped and turned to Perchik Rosenberg. "You're not my cousin or my friend. You will regret it if you do not let go of my arm."

With that, Rosenberg turned and walked briskly toward an older couple, who appeared to be lost and confused.

Looking around, Israel saw a line of people waiting to ask a government official for help. He waited, but not patiently. Israel was desperately eager to see the famous city on the way to his destination.

At last he reached the agent. Israel showed the man the note he had prepared. It said "225 Rivington Street between Allen and Franklin." He was told to take the subway and given the name of the station where he was to get off. The address Israel was given came from Lev Fineberg, the man he had met in Warsaw. Lev's cousin Saul lived on Rivington, in the heart of the Jewish neighborhood in New York's Lower East Side.

The agents in the subway station nearest to the ferry boats were well accustomed to helping immigrants, telling the "greenhorns" that a ride on the subway would cost them five cents and how to find the station where they were to get off. Israel walked to the subway station. Remembering what Perchik Rosenberg said about the subway "flying like a tornado underground," he hesitated before climbing down the stairs. Seeing that the crowds going down including many women and children, he followed them.

When he reached the platform he thought, "Oh, I see, this is just a train going through a tunnel." But he soon saw it was different, when the doors opened and the crowd poured out, while simultaneously the group he was standing with rushed and pushed their way into the car. The doors snapped close. The subway car shot out of the station, with many of the people standing and holding on to poles and straps. The inside of the tunnel flew by in a way that was nothing like looking at farmland from the window of a train.

After the third stop Israel found a seat and began to relax a little. But he noted that when people reached their stations they had to push their way through the hordes to reach the doors in time to get off. He was fascinated and distracted by the variety of humanity riding the subway—so much so, he nearly forgot to get up in time for his stop at the Delancey-Allen Street Station.

By the time he arrived there it was dark, had grown colder, and there was a light dusting of snow. Carrying his heavy suitcase, Israel hurried down Delancey to Rivington Street, anxious to reach a place of comfort and warmth. In his mind he fantasized Saul Fineberg as a friendly, generous man who would greet Israel as if he was a member of his own family.

There it was at last, number 225. As he climbed the steps to the old brownstone apartment house, Israel was cheering himself in anticipation. He was thinking about how Lev Fineberg's cousin would surely help him find a good place to live.

Israel rang the bell several times before someone came to the door. A tiny white-haired old woman wearing the wig of an orthodox Jew opened the door and looked at Israel suspiciously. She asked belligerently, "*Vas vilst du?*" (What do you want?) Hearing Yiddish spoken comforted Israel, even though the woman's demeanor was not friendly.

He explained that he had just arrived from the old country and was told to contact Saul Fineberg. "Oh, a greenhorn," she said. "Well, Mister greenhorn. Last week, your friend Saul Fineberg moved away in the middle of the night without paying his rent and only God knows where he is now."

Stunned by the news, Israel just stood still for several minutes, not knowing what to do next. The old woman, Bessie Lefkowitz, the owner of the building, was growing impatient. A woman who had experienced more of the downside of humanity than their better nature, she had become hardened. Her first instinct was to distrust any new person who came along.

But the pitiful look on Israel's face when he heard the news about Saul Fineberg touched the small vein of empathy still existing within her. She looked at her young visitor, then said, "Oy, Oy, Oy!" and opened the door wide, motioning for Israel to come into the house. She asked, "So, *boychik* (little boy), what will you do now?"

Setting his suitcase down and enjoying the warmth of the house and the faint fragrance of Jewish cooking, Israel replied, "I don't know. Do you have any rooms to rent? I have a little bit of money."

Softening when she heard he had some money, Bessie said, "All my rooms are rented, but I have a tenant who you can share a room with. Do you want to do that?"

"Yes, Mrs. ...? That would be good." At this point anything would have been acceptable to Israel.

"Lefkowitz, I'm the widow of Sam Lefkowitz, of blessed memory. He was a good man...been gone four years this month. He left me this house, so you see, he took care of me in my old age. That's a good man, isn't it?"

Israel nodded in agreement.

"So now I'm going to talk to Koplowitz about you sharing his room."

Mrs. Lefkowitz climbed the stairs and knocked on a door. No answer. She knocked again and yelled, "Koplowitz, I know you are in there. I got something important to tell you." Still there was no answer. "Koplowitz, you want I should have you thrown out?"

The door opened and Koplowitz appeared wearing what Mrs. Lefkowitz would deem a very fancy bathrobe. A big smile on his face, Koplowitz greeted his landlady cheerfully, saying, "Mrs. Lefkowitz, you are looking especially lovely today. So how can I help you?"

Ignoring his compliment, Mrs. Lefkowitz declared, "I got a greenhorn right off the boat's going to be your roommate."

"I don't want a roommate. Tell him to go away."

"Koplowitz, I haven't seen a penny from you in two months. You got a choice. Take in the greenhorn who has some rent money or go live on the street."

"You say he has rent money? I don't want a greenhorn, but alright, send him up. I'll look him over."

Mrs. Lefkowitz yelled downstairs, "Get your bag and come upstairs, greenhorn." Still yelling, she asked, "What's your name?"

Israel grabbed his bag and yelled, "Singer, Israel Singer."

Israel climbed up the stairs as Bessie Lefkowitz came down. As they passed, she commented, "Go see Koplowitz for your room. He's a little meshuga, but you know what? Everybody likes him! I do too, but don't tell him I said that!"

When he reached the top of the stairs, the man was waiting for him and said, "Your name is Israel? You don't look like an Israel to me. You look more like an Izzy. So, Izzy, schlep your bag into the room. I'll show you where you can sleep, then I'm going out to see a certain luscious lady…maybe two luscious ladies."

Israel thought to himself, "Izzy, I think I like that name… I can be Izzy Singer, my new name for my new life in my new country."

Izzy unpacked a few of his things and dropped them on the cot in an alcove of the room that was to be his. He threw his clothes off and got under the rough old blanket. Despite all that had happened that day, the moment he closed his eyes his body gave into his complete exhaustion and he slept more deeply than he had on any night of his journey.

Chapter 25

The *Luftmensch*

The next morning, Israel opened his eyes to a startling vision. His hairy roommate was totally nude and looking down at him with a broad, toothy smile.

Half awake, Israel heard, "Get up, Izzy. I'm going to show you the wonders of our world and the wild animals who wander our streets."

Israel woke and found his way down the hall to the bathroom, where he took a cold, energizing shower. When he returned to the room, Koplowitz was dressed and ready to go. Izzy dressed quickly and followed him down to the street. There he discovered that Vladimir "Koppy" Koplowitz was a *luftmensch*[6]. Israel had heard the term, but hadn't really understood exactly what it meant until he encountered Koplowitz; it was a Yiddish word for an impractical, contemplative person having no definite business or income. *Luft* means "air" and *mensch* means "man." So literally, a man who lives on air.

During the next two weeks he learned how a luftmensch lives as he observed his roommate's comings and goings. Koppy, though he had no specific job, had many talents and interests. He was an artist, a musician, a sign painter, a poet, a philosopher, and a card-carrying Communist. He could build and fix things with his hands and tell amazing stories he made up as he went along. Well known in the neighborhood, he had many friends. Each day he walked down Rivington Street to Delancey Street, greeting his friends along the way. Invariably someone would offer him a little job.

Beryl Spike, the kosher butcher, asked, "Koppy, can you paint me a sign? We got a special on tongue!"

"I'll bring it back later. Just write down what you want to say."

A woman called down from her window on the third floor, "Koppy, my dear, can you fix my kitchen chair for a nice meal and a bottle of beet borscht I'll give you to take home?" It was the widow, Mrs. Cohen.

"Alright, Mrs. Cohen, but can I bring along my greenhorn boarder just off the boat too?"

---

[6] A Yiddish word for an impractical, contemplative person having no definite business or income. *Luft* means air and *mensch* means a man—literally a man who lives on air.

"Yes, both of you come up later. I'll make some extra *kreplach* (dumplings)."

Walking down the street, a young mother was pushing a buggy with her baby girl inside. Her two little boys were poking along behind. The larger of the two boys was thin, pale, and sickly. The woman stopped and said, "Koppy, I'm so glad to I ran into you. My Moyshele is going to be five years old next week." Then she whispered in his ear, "My angel is very sick. The doctor said he doesn't know if Moyshele will live another year." Choking back tears, she continued, "I want to have a wonderful party for him. I heard about what you did for Frume Steinberg's little girl. I can pay you maybe half a dollar. I've been saving up. It's next Sunday at one o'clock. Can you tell stories and sing some songs for the children?"

"I'll be there. It will be my present for Moyshele. Save your money for the medicine."

Next, Koppy took Izzy to a theater on Second Avenue and said, "I'm going to see if Mr. Neshkin at the Yiddish Theater needs anything. I feel lucky today…like I'm going to be able to make some good money."

Koppy led Izzy through an alley to the theater's backstage entrance. The guard asked, "Who is that guy with you, Koppy?"

"This is my friend Izzy, just off the boat from Poland. I'm showing him around. Is Neshkin here? I want to see if he needs any help."

"Yes, he's here. Go to his office. You know where it is."

Just then, a worried-looking white-haired man who turned out to be Neshkin appeared and said, "Koppy, am I glad to see you! We have Thomashevsky's new play opening tonight and Yossel hasn't finished painting the scenery. I'll give you three dollars if you can help him finish in time. Who is the young man with you? Can he paint?"

Koppy answered, "Can he paint? This is my friend Izzy Singer, the famous Polish artist. He can paint anything you want. Isn't that so, Izzy?"

Izzy was startled by the sudden turn of events but had the presence of mind to declare, "Yes, whatever you want, I can paint it." He had never once held a paintbrush.

Neshkin said, "Alright, go to the stage. Tell Yossel I sent you. Another dollar and a half for the Polish kid, but hurry!"

Izzy was surprised to see what a skillful artist Koppy was. He painted details and shading expertly, so that if you stepped back a few feet everything looked real. Izzy was just asked to paint large areas of solid colors and was soon working his way rapidly across a blue sky panel.

They finished at 7:20 p.m. The paint was still wet when the great Boris Thomashevsky took the stage at 8 p.m. An experienced actor, he was accustomed to working with wet paint and costumes held together with safety pins on opening night.

As they headed back home in the dark they remembered Mrs. Cohen's meal offer and wondered if they might still be able get the food she had offered, even though it was late. They were hungry.

When they climbed the stairs to her apartment Mrs. Cohen greeted them warmly. With the recent loss of her husband, she loved having men in her apartment and made a fuss over them as she served them soup with kreplach, chopped liver, and freshly baked challah. Koppy looked over the chair that needed repairs and told Mrs. Cohen he would have it ready in a couple of days.

Izzy thought about all that had happened that day as they neared their Rivington Street apartment. His thoughts were interrupted when he heard some shouting coming from across the street.

"It's that damned gang of Irish thugs looking for trouble again," Koppy declared. "I see there are five of them picking on the two Adelstein boys. What do you think, Izzy? Should we make the odds a little better?"

Chapter 26

The Bullies

"Hey, you, kid—yeah, I'm talking to you. Let me see that funny little hat on your head." With that, short stocky Jimmy, the redheaded gang member who appeared to be the leader, pulled the yarmulke off Aaron Adelstein's head and threw it to one of the other gang members. The gang members laughed as they played keep away with the yarmulke, and Aaron tried desperately to retrieve his hat.

One member of the gang dropped it on the ground and stepped on it. Then he picked it up and handed it to Jimmy, who yelled, "Come get your funny hat, *sheeny* (a derogatory name for a Jew). I won't hurt you." Turning to the others, he remarked, "Not much."

The younger Adelstein brother, Yakov, yelled, "Leave us alone. We never did anything to you."

"Oh, is that so, Christ killer? You killed Jesus and our priest says you make your matzoh stuff with the blood of our kids. Isn't that right, guys?"

The gang members nodded in agreement.

Aaron spoke up, saying, "What are you talking about? Where did you get such ideas?"

"It's all in this book. It's called the 'Potocalls' or something like that."

"You mean that pack of lies called the 'Protocols of the Elders of Zion.' You actually believe that garbage?"

"Are you calling our priest a liar?" Pounding his fist in his hand and throwing Aaron's yarmulke away, he shouted, "Hey guys, what do we do to kikes who call our priest a liar?"

The bullies were speaking to the Adelstein brothers in English. Izzy didn't understood the words as he and Koppy approached. But when Izzy saw what looked like trouble, he reached in his pocket and pulled out his leather cutting tool. Seeing the sharp blade, Koppy said, "Put that away."

"Why? We can scare them away with this."

"Izzy, you don't understand. If we did that they would come back with clubs and knives and then, God forbid, guns. Pretty soon we would be in a regular war. There's a better way to handle this. Let's see what we can do."

The gang was getting ready to beat up the Adelstein brothers when Koppy and Izzy walked into the midst of the scene.

Jimmy glared at them and warned, "Go away. This is none of your business."

Up until this moment, throughout the day, Koppy had been conversing with everyone they encountered in Yiddish. While they were all Jewish, they were immigrants from different countries. It didn't matter if they were from Russia, Poland, Hungary, or even England, they all spoke and understood Yiddish.

But now, Koppy answered Jimmy in his heavily Russian-accented English, "Oh, but it is. You see, this is our street and these two fine young men are our friends. I think you kids got lost, didn't you? You don't belong on our street. Why don't you just go home and stay there."

Jimmy, the short leader of the gang, hitching himself up to his full height, said, "Mister, what if we don't want to go back to our street? What are you going to do about it? You don't look so tough to me."

"Oh, me? I'm plenty tough enough, but you're going to have to deal with my friend Izzy here. He just got out of prison. He's the famous Killer Izzy. Maybe you read about him in the papers. You can read, can't you? He's killed three men—of course, all in self-defense... Isn't that so, Izzy?"

Everyone was staring at Izzy, who turned to Koppy and asked what he had just said. Koppy pulled Izzy back a few feet and quickly whispered what he had just said to the gang. Izzy was shocked, and frantically asked, "Why did you say that?"

Koppy answered quickly, "I don't know. It's all I could come up with. Don't worry, I'll think of something!"

Koppy was full of imagination. He functioned on instinct, unaffected first impulse, and inventiveness.

But Izzy understood what Koppy was trying to do. He turned around, stepped forward, summoned his best scowl, and leveled his steadiest tough guy stare into the eyes of the gang leader. He concentrated on showing no trace of fear.

But actually, at that moment he was thinking of many things. First, he was disappointed to learn there were anti-Semites, even here in America. Then he thought about all the times he would have liked to have been able to avenge the insults to his friends and family visited upon them by the anti-Semites in Poland.

The air was filled with tension and danger. It was a stalemate. No one moved.

Just at that moment, Mr. Pinchas Adelstein and his oldest son came home from work. Seeing what was going on, Aaron's older brother picked up yarmulke and gave it to him. The father and son lined up next to the two younger brothers. A moment later, three more men emerged from the closest apartment house and then other men from the neighborhood gathered. Soon the gang was surrounded.

It was then that Koppy spoke, softly but with great conviction. "We really don't want to see anyone get hurt. Do we, men? So we have some good advice. Turn around and go back to your neighborhood and make sure you don't ever come back to this street again. Because if we see you here again, it won't end so nicely."

Jimmy looked around slowly, turned, and motioned for the gang to follow him. They walked away.

Koppy smiled at Izzy, saying, "We did good, didn't we Killer Izzy?"

They shook hands and laughed.

Chapter 27

Three Busy Weeks and a Letter to Losice

Over the next twenty days, under the tutelage of Koppy the luftmensch, Izzy was exposed to a dizzying array of experiences. He met many of the neighborhood's eccentric characters, who gravitated naturally to Koppy. There was Leo Levine, an ardent Communist who would grab hold of your lapel and spout quotations from the "Communist Manifesto." He would only let go if you promised to come to a meeting. At Spike's kosher butcher shop, where Koppy stopped to drop off the sign he had painted, the three Spike brothers, Aaron, Beryl, and Chaim, were always arguing and threatening one another with their sharpened knives and cleavers. Koppy called them the "*Aleph Bet Gimmel* brothers" (ABC in Hebrew). If he visited them and they weren't fighting one another, Koppy would playfully try to goad them into an argument…like the time he told Beryl that Chaim and Aaron had called him stingy and selfish, just to see what would happen. Knives and cleavers flew!

One day Koppy confessed to Izzy, "I'm in love with the beautiful identical Finklestein twins, Bertha and Bessie."

Izzy asked, "Both of them? How can you be in love with both of them?"

He answered, "How can I not? I can't tell them apart."

Koppy showed Izzy as much of life in the city as he could. He was getting pleasure playing the role of tour guide. But he didn't limit the territory to the better neighborhoods. Koppy also had connections in the poverty-plagued areas. On one occasion they visited a family on the fifth floor of a shabby tenement building. A family of twelve lived in a two-room apartment. There was only one water faucet and one bathroom for all the apartments on the fifth floor, which was reached by a dark stairwell. The children were malnourished and the parents spent all day and half the night sewing in a sweatshop for starvation wages.

The streets teemed with carts pushed by peddlers hawking everything from fruits and vegetables to elixirs promising to cure all ailments from lumbago to ingrown toenails.

Izzy compared the quality of life in New York's Jewish neighborhood to his home in Losice. In the city it was incredibly crowded, noisy, and filled with Jews trying desperately to claw their way out of poverty. So, the question was, Why did they come here? Izzy pondered that question and discussed it with Koppy.

"So, Izzy Singer, what did you expect to find in America…streets paved with gold? No, there are no such streets here. But there is one thing you will find here that you could never find in your shtetl."

"And what is that?" Izzy responded, already believing he knew the answer.

"In English it's called 'hope.' You can hope for a better life and know that it is possible, because you do not have the *goyim's* (non-Jews) boots on your neck!"

"Koppy, I understand what you are saying, but this does not feel like a place of hope for me."

"Yes, I know what you mean. Sometimes I feel like I want to go to another place in America. This is a very big country. But I don't have the kind of nerve it takes to leave this place."

"But if you could leave, you would. Where would you go?"

Koppy thought for a moment, then replied, "Not north to Boston. No, I would go west, to Pittsburgh or Detroit or Chicago or someplace like that."

"What have you heard about Cleveland?"

"Cleveland? I think that would be a good choice. Why do you ask?"

"I have just enough money to get there."

That night Izzy wrote a letter to Losice.

Dear Papa and Mama,

This is the first time I could write to you. I hope you are well. Don't worry about me. Many things happened to me, but I am alright. In America they call me Izzy Singer. I think I like that.

The boat trip to America was very hard. I hope you come here someday. But you must not come in steerage like I did. It's not a good way.

The man I was to meet in New York moved away. I am living in a house with a man named Koplowitz. I call him Koppy. Most people on our street speak Yiddish. I want to learn English. There is kosher food here and a shul called Beth Shalom near me.

The city is big, with wonderful things. I see many motor cars and trucks. I ride on a train that goes fast under the ground and one that rides on rails up in the sky. There is a new machine here called a Victrola that makes music. When people have enough money they buy one. They play it all the time. I hear music coming from every house. Many homes have pianos. Children take piano lessons. Koppy says it is a waste of money.

Koppy has been showing me the neighborhood. There are too many people here. It is hard to get work because there are so many people looking for work. The pay is very little. I have seen bad things here in this Jewish place in New York City. Some people have Victrolas and pianos, but most people are very poor. They are crowded into small apartment houses. Many children and old people are sick. They don't have enough food to eat. There are organizations that try to help them, but there are so many people they can only help a few of them.

I wanted to try to make a living here in New York, but it is so hard to find work, I decided to go to the city called Cleveland. I have the name of a man to see when I get there. I will go on a train tomorrow. I will write to you from Cleveland.

Your loving son,

Israel

Chapter 28

Good-bye New York, Hello Cleveland

Izzy Singer rose early in the morning. As he packed his suitcase, he was thinking about all that had happened in the past 3 months in New York and now he was ready for the next chapter in his great adventure.

It was time to say good-bye to Koppy and their landlady. Both were sorry to see him leave and wished him well. Bessie Lefkowitz said, "Izzy, here is a bag with some mandel broit and rugelach for my favorite greenhorn…oh, and a shtickle halvah. Enjoy them on your trip, boychik." She kissed his cheek.

Koppy slapped Izzy on the back as he declared, "Look out, Cleveland! Killer Izzy is coming!" Izzy and Koppy looked at one another bittersweetly…like friends who met at summer camp, had wonderful and crazy adventures together they knew they would never forget, and now they would never meet again.

Izzy took the subway to Grand Central Terminal to board the New York Central train bound for Chicago, via Pittsburgh and Cleveland. The view from his train window was a rolling cascade of scenery: first, New York and New Jersey urban landscapes, then as the train moved into Pennsylvania, mountainous areas, forests, and farms. As he gazed out the window, Izzy thought about all that had happened to him since he left home and felt more than a twinge of homesickness. Then his thoughts turned to his destination. He wondered, "What will Cleveland be like? Will I find a good job? Will the man whose name I was given be there or will he have disappeared like the man in New York?"

The hours passed. He fell asleep until the train stopped in Pittsburgh, where many passengers left the train and new ones boarded. Three more hours passed and finally he heard the train conductor call out "Cleveland."

What he didn't know was that Solomon Goldman, the man whose name was given to Izzy, had been sent a letter from Lev Fineberg. It read as follows:

Dear Solomon,

I hope this letter finds you in good health and that your business is continuing to prosper. I want you to know that a young man named

Israel Zynger from the shtetl Losice in Poland may be coming to Cleveland and contacting you soon. He is an ambitious young man from a good family and he is a good leather-worker. I would appreciate whatever assistance you can give to Israel. He worked hard and proved his skill in his uncle's shoe-making factory.

I expect to be making a business trip to Cleveland in two months.

Best wishes from your friend,

Lev

Pinhas Slobodnik was Solomon Goldman's widowed sister Hannah's only child. A handsome man in his early twenties with a head of dark wavy hair, Pinhas had been spoiled by his overprotective parents. He was seldom denied anything he asked for, from the time he was a small child; he had developed the sense that he was entitled to whatever he wanted, without any obligation to work for it.

Solomon loved his nephew and though he had his doubts that Pinhas would be of any use in his fur business, he employed the young man, hoping he might develop some kind of skill, either as a furrier or as a marketer of fur coats. Though he constantly expressed his thanks to his uncle for employing him, Pinhas made little effort to actually be productive and often took days off for whatever diversions met his fancy.

The only aspect of the business that interested him was the financial records. One afternoon, secretly perusing the company's bank statement, his eyes grew wide. Up until that moment he had no realistic idea of how much money his uncle was making. He saw large figures in the statements and erroneously concluded that they represented enormous profits. (Actually, he was looking at the figures for gross sales and not net profits.)

From that moment, a plan began to develop in his mind. His uncle had no children, so Pinhas was certain he would inherit the business. He knew his ability to actually run the business profitably was not a good bet. Plan A was that after his uncle died he would find someone who could run the company for him. Failing that, Plan B was to sell the business and live the rest of his life on the money it brought. He thought, "That way I won't ever have to engage in the inconvenience of actually pretending to work."

Solomon Goldman was out of town when the aforementioned letter arrived, so the envelope was opened and read by Pinhas. He had an uneasy feeling when he read it. He worried that any talented, hardworking newcomer could be a threat to his ambition to take over his aged uncle's business.

He didn't dare destroy the letter, though. Instead he hid it in the back of a seldom-used compartment of his uncle's roll-top desk. He planned to feign no knowledge of how it got there if it was ever discovered.

Chapter 29

Mathilda

Israel arrived in Cleveland the week of Rosh Hashana. He found his way to the Woodland Avenue neighborhood where most of the Jews lived and where he could find the Yiddish speakers who might help him find a place to live. He also felt certain Solomon Goldman must be located in that area.

It was on East 38th Street and Scovill Avenue near Congregation *Oheb Zedek* (Lovers of Righteousness) that Israel saw a sign reading "Rooms to Let" in both English and Yiddish. Schlepping his big suitcase, he climbed the stairs of the wood-frame two-story home.

Answering his knock on the door was an attractive auburn-haired middle-age woman named Mathilda Garson. Mathilda, recently widowed, was a buxom woman with the kind of curvaceous figure that causes men's eyes to follow her down the street. Mathilda looked Israel over, smiled charmingly, and asked, "Are you interested in renting a room, young man? I have three rooms available. One is on the first floor for ten dollars a month and two on the second floor for eight dollars."

Israel said, "Thank you. Please excuse me. I need to count my money." Pulling his money out of his pocket, he counted it very carefully as Mathilda watched hopefully. As a recent widow, she needed to find lodgers as soon as she could to help pay her bills. But as she gazed at the strong and healthy-looking young man another thought crossed her mind, causing her to momentarily blush.

Israel liked the look of the house and couldn't help noticing the warmth in the woman's greeting. But after counting his money, which had dwindled since leaving New York, he shook his head, saying, "Do you have any other rooms, for perhaps a little less?"

The widow Garson thought for a moment. A smile crossing her face, she said, "If you are willing to do a little work to get it ready, I think I can let you have the attic for five dollars a month. But I'll tell you what. You won't have to do that work right away. You can stay in the room next to mine on the first floor until I rent it to someone else. That might happen tomorrow or in a week or two, I don't know. What do you think, Mister…?"

"My name is Israel Singer, but everyone in America calls me Izzy. Yes, that sounds good to me, but do you mean I will only have to pay five dollars a month even while I'm living in the ten-dollar room?"

"Izzy Singer, what a nice name! You're new in America. Where are you from?"

"I have come here from the shtetl Losice in Poland. But I want to be an American."

"And so, you will be Izzy Singer. My name is Mathilda Garson. And yes, about the rent, that is what I mean."

"That is very kind, but it seems unfair for you, so if you will permit me I would like to help you out in any way I can."

"Oh, my, that would be wonderful. I think you may be able to help me in ways you may not imagine. Just bring your suitcase into that room over there. And after you have unpacked, come into the parlor, where we can make the arrangements, have some tea, and get better acquainted."

Having said that, Mathilda, unable to resist the temptation, reached out and touched Izzy's cheek, saying, "Welcome to my home, Izzy Singer."

Chapter 30

Rosh Hashana

Rosh Hashana, the Jewish New Year of 1907, turned out to be a watershed day in the life of Izzy Singer. The events that occurred from early in the day until late that night would never be forgotten.

"S. Goldman, Furrier" was located just two blocks from Mathilda Garson's house on East 40th Street. Solomon Goldman had gone to Detroit, where he was visiting a cousin. He wanted to get back in time for Rosh Hashana services. A short, thin white-haired man, Solomon had a special air about him. Everyone who knew him knew he was competent, wise, and trustworthy. He had come to America from Lithuania in 1872 with nothing but skill at leather-working and a powerful ambition to make it in America.

And now, in 1907, he had realized his dream. He owned a small factory with ten employees and his regular customers were some of Cleveland's finest stores. But the early days of privation in Europe and the strain of working fourteen-plus-hour days for years had taken a serious toll on his health.

Business-wise, he had finally begun to make a decent profit, but was by no means wealthy. He felt that his business had reached a point where, with just a little more hard work, it could turn a corner and become really prosperous. But just at this key moment his health was failing. What he needed more than anything else was someone who was adequately skilled and experienced to help him through this time of maximum opportunity. His nephew Pinhas was never going to be that person.

The first day of Rosh Hashana was a warm and sunny day in Cleveland. Virtually every Jew in the area would be dressed up in their finest and out on the street heading for services at their chosen synagogue. People who hadn't seen one another since Yom Kippur of the previous year were making small talk and discussing the merits of the various rabbis, cantors, and choirs.

Solomon was a longtime member of Oheb Zedek. He had made a special High Holy Days donation to the synagogue and was looking forward to this Rosh Hashana service with great anticipation and pride.

Mathilda Garson also belonged to Oheb Zedek and brought her new tenant Izzy along. Izzy picked up a Talit, said the prayer for donning it, and sat down in the back row. As was orthodox tradition, Mathilda climbed the stairs to the balcony and sat with the other women, looking down at the proceedings from the balcony.

During a lull in the service, Izzy turned to the man seated next to him, introduced himself, and said, "I am Izzy Singer and I am new here in Cleveland. Do you know many of the people here?"

The man said, "My name is Karp, Hyman Karp, and yes, I do. I have lived here many years. Is there anyone in particular you are looking for?"

"Have you ever met a man named Solomon Goldman?"

"I never met him, but I know what he looks like. He should be here today. I will point him out to you when I see him."

The service continued. Izzy was impressed with both the rabbi and the cantor, who had a beautiful voice filled with the little sobbing touches he had heard back home from the Losice cantor.

It was time for the Torah service. The ark was opened. There were three beautiful Torahs in it, each with shiny silver breastplates and crowns with little bells and pointers hanging from silver chains. They were paraded throughout the synagogue. As they passed Izzy touched one with his Talit and kissed it.

One of the Torahs was selected for the reading. The ornaments and velvet cover were removed. The Torah was laid down on the table and opened to the portion of the week. The first man came up to perform his Aliyah. Izzy asked Hyman Karp to tell him the names of readers. He wanted to learn the names of as many people as possible.

"Horowitz...Yes, that's Horowitz!" The next man was Friedman, and then Lavenstein. Then Karp said, "There he is!"

"There who is?"

"Why, it's Goldman, Solomon Goldman is doing the fourth Aliyah. That's quite an honor!"

Solomon Goldman paused for a moment before he began the prayer that precedes the Torah reading. He gazed out at the congregation, savoring the moment; this was the first time he had been able to donate enough money to the congregation to be afforded such an honor. Then he began the prayer he remembered from the time of his Bar Mitzvah, a lifetime ago in Lithuania: *"Boruchu es Adonai ha mvorach..."*

The service went on for several hours. Afterward, Izzy left the synagogue and waited near the large entrance doors until he saw Solomon Goldman leaving with a woman and a young man. Several people spoke to Goldman wishing him a *"L'shana tova tikvah tayvu"* (May you be written in the book of life for a good year) and congratulating him on the honor of his Aliyah prayer.

Izzy waited patiently until the crowd dispersed. Then he walked up to Mr. Goldman. Gathering his courage and all the chutzpah he could garner, he said, "Mr. Goldman, my name is Izzy Singer. I came to Cleveland from

Poland because I was given your name by my friend Lev Fineberg."

But before he could continue, Pinhas Slobodnik stepped between his uncle and Izzy. (He had just realized that the Israel Zynger mentioned in the letter from Lev Feinberg was this same person who now called himself Izzy Singer.) Desperate to keep this possible rival away, he said, "My uncle is very tired and doesn't have time to talk now." Then he turned, locked his uncle's arm in his, and started to walk toward their homes.

Izzy was left standing there, wondering what had just happened and why. He stood watching. Then he decided to follow the Goldmans, to see where they lived. After the Goldmans walked half a block, Solomon stopped and turned to his nephew, saying, "You were right, Pinhas. I am tired. But not so tired that I should be rude to a man who was sent here by my good friend Lev Fineberg. Go find that young man and ask him to please come here. I want to talk to him."

Pinhas said, "Oh, I'm sure he has gone away. I wouldn't know where to find him."

Solomon Goldman turned around, saw Izzy standing a short distance behind them, and angrily turned to his nephew.

"Look, he's right there behind us, you fool. Now go and fetch him."

Pinhas, having no choice, walked slowly back to where Izzy stood and said, "My uncle wants to talk to you. But don't take up too much of his time. He's an old man and not very well."

When they both joined Solomon Goldman, the old man said, "Please forgive my nephew. He has the idea that I'm going to die any minute and is trying to protect me. So, you say you are from the shtetl Losice. What did you do there?"

"I was a leather-worker. I worked for my uncle, Avrum Binstock, in his shoe-making factory."

Nodding his head, Solomon asked, "Do you have any experience with fur?"

"Yes, I do, I made some fur hats and a fur coat my uncle liked so much he bought it for himself. I enjoy working with fur."

His answer was an honest one. On one market day back in Losice, as Israel was strolling through the stalls, he came upon a display of rabbit and beaver fur pelts brought in by a local trapper. He had become skilled at working with leather in making shoes and thought he might try using his skills as a furrier. He had also recently been schooled in the art of bargaining by his uncle Avrum and thought this would be a good time to try the techniques he had learned. Noting that at the moment he seemed to be the only person who had any interest in the pelts, Israel made an offer for them that was one half of the asking price. The trapper scoffed at his offer, so Israel walked away. Just as he was about to leave the market place he felt a tap on his shoulder. It was the trapper who said, "Come back to my stall. I'm certain we can come to an agreement." They bargained for several minutes. The result was that the trapper accepted his offer after Israel offered to repair the trapper's boots as part of the deal.

Israel had a friend who was a furrier. He gave Israel some tips and loaned him some patterns. At night, after working all day in the shoe factory Israel set about making a muff for his mother and two fur hats. They came out so well he started work on a full length beaver coat. When he finished it he showed it to Avrum who was so impressed he declared, "Israel, I would like to buy that coat for myself. I will be proud to wear it."

Israel would have had no way of knowing at that time that his furrier venture would one day be the key to realizing all his dreams.

"Pinhas, do you have some paper and a pencil? Yes? Write down the address of Solomon Goldman Company and give it to Izzy here. Izzy Singer, please come to my place of business Monday morning at seven and we'll find out just how good a leather-worker you are."

With that said, Solomon, his sister, and an unhappy Pinhas turned and walked home. Izzy felt elated as he looked at the piece of paper scribbled with the address 2040 W. 40th Street.

He then headed home, to Mathilda Garson's home on East 38th Street. When he arrived, Mathilda came out of her room to greet him. He shared with her what had just happened with Solomon Goldman and how he was looking forward to showing him what he could do. But Mathilda wanted to talk about Rosh Hashana.

Mathilda said, "Come, Izzy. Let's sit down in the parlor and talk about Rosh Hashana. That was a beautiful service today, don't you think? But it was a little long, because today is also Shabbat. It is unusual for Rosh Hashana to be on the Shabbat. Would you like a little glass of schnapps to celebrate the holiday?"

"Why, yes," Izzy replied. He was surprised. No woman had ever offered him a shot before.

Matilda got the bottle and two shot glasses. She poured the drinks and, picking hers up, said, "L'Chaim." They both downed their drinks.

They sat quietly for a few minutes. Matilda poured two more drinks. This time Izzy said, "L'Chaim."

They were both beginning to feel the effects of their drinks. Then, feeling relaxed and uninhibited, Matilda said, "Did you know that it is considered a *mitzvah* (good deed) to make love on the Shabbat, and a double mitzvah if the Shabbat is on the first day of Rosh Hashana?"

"No, I didn't know. That's very interesting."

"My husband, Ben, of blessed memory, and I loved to do that mitzvah every Shabbat."

Izzy, feeling uncomfortable with the conversation, blushed and said, "I'm sure you must miss him."

"Oh, Izzy darling, how sweet of you to say that. You are a very understanding young man. Do you mind if I give you a hug? I really miss not having anyone to hug."

"A hug? Why...no."

They were sitting on the big overstuffed brown mohair sofa. Mathilda moved closer and put her arms around Izzy, who felt surprised, confused, and excited all at once. He reacted by encircling Mathilda with his arms.

The hug lasted longer than expected, and Izzy felt Mathilda's warm breasts press against his body. Both of them were breathing hard. Finally they released the hug and Mathilda said, "Think of it...missing a chance for a double mitzvah." Softly, under her breath, she said, "Maybe I don't need to miss that chance." The fact that the mitzvah was only supposed to apply to married couples was something Mathilda Garson would not be concerned about now.

She stood up and looked into Izzy's eyes with a gaze he would long remember. Before she turned to leave she said, "It's been a long day. I think I'll get ready for bed."

When Mathilda returned to her room she was in a high state of arousal and quickly undressed, washed, and perfumed her body. These thoughts floated through her mind: "I wonder why this Izzy has such an effect on me. Is it because...I think he may never have...and I would be the first. That's exciting...but do I dare?"

It had been a long and eventful day. Izzy quickly undressed and got under the covers, but he couldn't fall asleep. He lay in bed listening to the sounds of the night: a far off train, someone in the street shouting, a dog barking. Finally, at about eleven his eyes began to close. It was then that he heard a click at his door.

It opened and in the faint light of the moon coming through his window he saw Mathilda enter his room, wearing a nightgown. She stood looking at him for a moment, then walked to the side of his bed, where she realized he was awake and silently gazing at her. She removed her gown, letting it fall to the floor, and stood there naked as Izzy eyes grew wide. Then, in silence, she slipped into his bed.

Chapter 31

The Afterglow and the Frustration

Mathilda's suspicion about Izzy was confirmed. This was the first time for Izzy Singer and a night he would never forget as long as he still breathed.

The first thing Mathilda did when she entered the bed was to instruct Izzy to take off his night shirt. His arousal and excitement when he felt the buttery soft smoothness of Mathilda's naked body and was enveloped by her perfumed fragrance propelled him into a state of pure bliss. His member was immediately erect in anticipation of the pleasures and release to come, of which he had only heard from others.

Mathilda simultaneously kissed Izzy and put his hand on her breast. She reached down to his groin in order to ascertain his readiness and let out a delighted, "Oh, my!" with her discovery. But her touch, added to all of the arousal, caused him to spill his seed all over her hand and the bed. He groaned in dismay, but she only laughed and said, "Don't worry, I'm sure you have much more to give." And so he did....

Though he slept very little that night, Izzy awoke early the next morning with a smile on his face, a smile that would remain with him whenever he thought about that night.

But first: Monday morning, it was time to find his way to Solomon Goldman's place of business. When he arose he found Mathilda had returned to her own room and was deeply asleep. Izzy, with the slip of paper he was given the previous day by Pinhas, stepped out onto the street. It was about 6 a.m. He was looking for anyone who could tell him how to find the address he was given.

Seeing no one on the street, he walked to Woodland Avenue, where he was sure there would be some activity, even at this hour. There he saw a milkman on his delivery route with his horse-drawn cart. The milkman spoke no Yiddish, but understood what Izzy wanted to know and did his best to explain that a trolley car went to the public square, and from there he could get another trolley that would take him to West 40th Street by way of the Center Street Bridge.

Still with a smile on his face as he thought about the night he'd had, Izzy found the first and then the second trolley. It was ten minutes to seven when he reached West 40th.

He looked for the address. Izzy was anxious to make a good impression on Mr. Goldman and be on time at 7 a.m. There were more people on the street now, all going to work. He stopped one man and tried to ask him for directions in Yiddish, but there were no Yiddish speakers in the all-gentile neighborhood.

Then he noticed a Russian Orthodox Church. Like many neighborhoods in Cleveland, this one was ethnically concentrated into one specific group. Izzy had picked up a little Russian back in Losice, which was near the Russian border. He knew just enough to secure some basic information.

He stopped another man and tried his Russian. The man pointed south and Izzy headed that way on West 40th. He was surprised to discover that the street had nothing but homes on it. There were no businesses. Confused, he continued to the end of the street, which led into a cemetery. He couldn't understand how he had made such a mistake. The smile left his face as he realized he may have lost his one chance to make a business connection in Cleveland. Not knowing what else to do, he found his way back to Mathilda's house.

When he arrived, Mathilda was having her breakfast. She started to greet Izzy warmly but quickly noticed how upset he was. "Izzy, my darling," she cooed. "What's the matter? What happened at work?"

Nearly in tears, Izzy responded, "Nothing happened. I couldn't find the place. I don't understand why. I had the address but the place wasn't there. I wanted to make a good impression on Mr. Goldman and I couldn't even find his place. What will he think of me? He'll think I'm a regular *schlemiel*." (a fool)

"Izzy, you're not a schlemiel. Now tell me what happened. Maybe I can help."

Izzy described where he had been that morning. Mathilda listened attentively, then said, "Can I please see the address you were given?"

When she looked at the piece of paper she shook her head in disbelief. "Who gave you this?"

"Solomon Goldman's nephew gave it to me. Why do you ask?"

"Solomon Goldman's business is on *East* 40th street, not way out on West 40th, the other side of Cleveland. East 40th is about two blocks from here. You go there right now and show this note to Mr. Goldman. There is some kind of funny business going on with his nephew."

At the same time, in the office of the Goldman fur shop, Pinhas was talking to his uncle, saying, "It's too bad about that greenhorn. Oh, well, he probably found another job." Pinhas seldom thought much about the possible consequences of his actions, like what would happen if Izzy Singer came later and showed his obviously wrongly addressed note to his uncle.

Solomon Goldman was distressed that Izzy Singer hadn't shown up. Izzy had made a good impression on him and he was disappointed. In addition to his disappointment he was not feeling well. He had been feeling pain in his chest from time to time and often ran out of breath if he tried to walk briskly.

Izzy didn't stop to have breakfast, but he did take along a chicken sandwich Mathilda had made for him. He walked quickly to 2040 East 40th Street, arriving at Solomon Goldman's business at 8:45 a.m.

When Izzy arrived, Pinhas wasn't in the shop, but had gone home supposedly to help his mother with some task. Izzy, by that time, understood that Pinhas didn't like him, though he didn't know why. Knowing Pinhas was Goldman's nephew, Izzy had decided it might be best if could try to make friends with him. He determined that at least for the time being, he would keep the purposely wrongly addressed note to himself if he could do so and still get his chance to work for Goldman.

When he arrived he said, "Mr. Goldman!. I'm so sorry I'm late. I'm such a greenhorn. I lost my way here and got all mixed up. I'll stay late today to make up for the time I was late and don't worry, I know how to find my way now. What would you like me to do?"

Goldman was moved by Izzy's sincerity. He led him into the fur shop and said, "Here is a piece of Persian Lamb fur and a pattern for a muff. Let's see how well you cut it."

Goldman was impressed when he saw Izzy reach into his pocket and pull out his own very sharp leather-cutting tool, and even more impressed when he saw how quickly, confidently, and accurately Izzy finished the job. He was then given a series of other tasks, each a little more complex. It was obvious that Izzy was up to all the tasks.

Pinhas returned around noon. Seeing Izzy working in the shop, he was very surprised, and worried about what his uncle would say. He was sure Izzy would show him the note with the wrong address. But nothing was said about the address. Pinhas was astonished when Izzy greeted him with a smile.

At the end of the day, Solomon Goldman was very pleased with Izzy's work and said, "We will expect you tomorrow morning at 7 a.m. We will talk about your pay at that time."

Chapter 32

Solomon Goldman's Plan

Now, for the first time since he left home, Izzy Singer had regular employment. He viewed this as the real first step toward reaching his long-term goal of making enough money to bring his family to America. Solomon Goldman was obviously very pleased with his work, and he was getting along well with the other leather-workers, who quickly came to respect not only his skill, but also his diligence. He was always on time to work, never took more than half an hour for lunch, and frequently stayed late to finish work.

Pinhas was unhappy. He could imagine a scenario where Izzy would be promoted to a higher position and take away what he and his mother believed was rightly his. Pinhas was constantly trying to think of ways to undermine Izzy. But nothing he tried worked.

The days moved on into weeks and months…a year, then two, then four years passed. Solomon Goldman's health was failing. For the first time, he was leaving work early and staying home one or two days a week. As he did so, he became more and more dependent on Izzy, who was now the shop foreman.

Solomon, whose chest pain had been increasing, had been thinking about what he would do with the business when he would no longer be able to operate it. He devised a plan he was well aware would cause him grief from his family, mainly his sister and her worthless son Pinhas.

On this particular day in March, he asked Izzy to come into his office and said, "Izzy, you have become like a son to me, the son I never had. I worked very hard many years to build my business, but soon I won't be able to come to work anymore. I have come up with an idea." He paused and looked into Izzy's eyes. "How would you like to run the Solomon Goldman Company for me, and for someday it to belong to you?"

Izzy was astounded, but immediately answered in the affirmative.

Solomon said, "Good. I want to be fair to you, so here is what I propose. We will get a lawyer to draw up papers. As long as I am alive, you will pay an agreed-upon amount to me every month. After I die, you will pay that same amount to my sister for ten more years. Then the business will belong to you.

"I want you to go to my desk. There you will find all the papers with all the accounts. Clean out the desk and put all the papers on this table. I want to be certain we have everything…all the figures right, so everyone will be treated fairly. We will meet with the lawyer in two days."

Izzy, in an excited state, went to work immediately, emptying out the big old roll-top desk and sorting the papers: invoices, income statements, records of payment to employees, etc.

He had taken virtually everything out of the desk and placed it on a table when he spotted a small piece of paper jammed into the back of one of the small compartments. He unfolded it and read it. It was a letter from Lev Feinberg to Solomon Goldman about Izzy's expected arrival, dated in 1906.

That letter was the key to a minor mystery. Lev Feinberg had come to visit Goldman a month after Izzy started working at the fur shop. Lev was delighted to see Izzy working there and mentioned the letter he had written to Goldman, who didn't remember ever receiving it. As Izzy stared at the long-lost letter, he tried to figure out how the letter ended up hidden in the desk.

There was only one possible explanation, he thought: "More Pinhas mischief." Izzy folded up the letter and later put it together with the purposely wrong addressed note he had been given by Pinhas that first day four years earlier. He thought the two notes might come in handy someday.

Chapter 33

A Letter from Dorothy

And now we return to Mathilda. Four years earlier, when Izzy had first arrived in Cleveland and found himself in bed with his landlady, for the next several Shabbats, and many times during the week, Mathilda and Izzy enjoyed performing their "mitzvah."

But everything changed when one day a new tenant appeared. Sam Shapiro, a forty-eight-year-old, balding salesman for a local tool manufacturer had rented the first-floor room that had been occupied by Izzy.

Izzy was then banished to the attic room. Mathilda's attitude toward him changed overnight. He was good for pleasure, but Sam Shapiro, a jovial, charming man who loved to tell slightly "off color" jokes, looked like husband material to her.

Izzy naturally missed the sex, but he understood what was happening and why. Still, a few more times Mathilda and Izzy enjoyed a few hours together. But gradually, Mathilda put Sam under her spell and Izzy found himself abandoned by his lover. He grew increasingly uncomfortable in the situation. After working for Solomon Goldman for several months, he made enough money to rent a small apartment of his own. He also began to dream of having a woman in his life.

Ever since he left London, he had been thinking about that pretty red-haired girl Dorothy Greenbaum. He started a correspondence with her and soon they were writing to one another twice a month. The letters kept up with their lives and continued with the mundane matters of life—until in the fourth year, when Dorothy was sixteen, Izzy received the following:

Dear Israel,

You knew from my previous letter that my mother was ill with influenza, that terrible disease. We have been cursed by it. Two weeks ago my father Marvin succumbed and then my mother died three days later. My brothers Israel and Morris and I are devastated. How could this happen to our family?

These days are hard days, but the nights are worse. Many nights I can't sleep. I imagine I will lose my brothers Morris and Israel and be left alone in this world. I feel that God has forsaken us, but why? We have observed the commandments and done everything we could to be good Jews.

Life is so difficult, but we are doing the best we can to survive. Israel is married now and will soon be a father. Morris has a job and is bringing in a little money, and we have our family's home. But it is now a place of great sadness. We have dreamed of someday going to America, where we feel there will be better opportunities and we can start a new life.

You are the only person in America we know. If we move to Cleveland can you help us? I hate to have to ask you for this help, but I feel from our letters that we have made a strong connection. Do you feel that way too? We look forward to your reply as soon as you can write.

Sincerely,

Dorothy

Izzy felt very distressed when he read the letter. While in London he had spent two wonderful evenings in the Greenbaum home and had gotten to know and admire the family. And, of course, he had grown very fond of Dorothy. Her letter was heartbreaking. He wanted to reach out to her in any way he could, so he immediately wrote his reply:

Dear Dorothy,

Your letter shocked me. I can't imagine how you feel. I spent two evenings with your mother and father and I found them to be wonderful people. What a terrible loss you have suffered. My deeply felt condolences to you and your brothers.

The answer to your question is yes. I want to help you any way I can. Let me know when you plan to come. Do you have enough money to make the trip? Please, if possible, do not travel in steerage. It is very bad. I know because that is what I did.

I will find a place for you to live. You will like Cleveland. There are many Jewish people in this neighborhood who speak Yiddish, but you should be able to get along very well anywhere in America because you speak English. I am especially looking forward to seeing you now that you are sixteen years old and all grown up.

I look forward to your arrival and helping you make a happy new life in America.

With affection,

Israel

Chapter 34

The Family Meeting

David Finkelstein, Solomon's lawyer, met with Solomon and Izzy for several hours over two days and drew up an agreement that was satisfactory to both of them.

The following week, Solomon called his sister Hannah and his nephew Pinhas in for a meeting. He intended to tell them about the arrangement he had made. Izzy was at the meeting too.

The arrangement included a substantial guaranteed income for his relatives. Solomon felt confident they would be pleased. And so he broached the subject in a warm and pleasant way, saying, "Hannah and Pinhas, my loved ones, I have some good news for you. Since I am no longer well enough to run my business, I have arranged to sell it to Izzy over a period of years."

Hannah gasped and shouted, "What did you say? You are selling the business to the greenhorn? You are going to take it away from your own flesh and blood and give it to a stranger? How could you do such a thing?"

Pinhas whined, "I always thought you would give the business to me. I have been working so hard for you all these years and this is the way you treat me? What kind of an uncle are you? You let Izzy here poison your mind toward me, didn't you?"

Solomon was shocked by the outburst. He needed to sit down and calm himself. The pain in his chest returned. He turned to Izzy and said, "Izzy, please get me my pills and a glass of water." While he waited for the pills and water everyone was quiet. They were waiting to hear what he would say next. Solomon gathered his thoughts, slowly drank the glass of water, and began his response.

"Hannah and Pinhas, the first thing you need to know is that my mind is made up and the contract has been signed. I will tell you why I did it so maybe you will understand. I hope so.

"I have worked many years to build this business and I am very proud of what I did. I'm proud that I have been able to make jobs for many fine men.

"For years I have been worried about what would happen to my business when I got old and died. The doctor tells me I am a sick man. I don't know how much time I still have, but I don't think it's long."

Then, gazing into his nephew's eyes, he said, "I gave you every chance to show me you could take over the business, but you failed at every job you were given." Pinhas started to talk, but Solomon put up his hand to silence him.

Solomon continued, "Just when I had given up the thought that I would ever find someone who was able to do the job, Izzy came along. He has not only shown me he could run the business, but I believe he will be able make it grow. I'm so glad that he found his way to me. Hannah, you and Pinhas will benefit greatly from this arrangement and you won't have to do anything to earn all the money you will get after I die."

Hannah was crying and blew her nose. Pinhas clenched his fists in frustration and demanded, "Mother, aren't you going to say something?"

Hannah only wailed loudly as Solomon declared, "I'm sorry, but I'm not feeling well. I have to end this meeting." With that he left the office and had one of the workers take him home.

The sobbing Hannah followed him out the door as Pinhas turned to Izzy, saying, "You did this, didn't you? I'm not finished with you. You'll see!"

Izzy was calm. His retort was, "I have the evidence of those things you used to try to keep me away from your uncle four years ago. I have never shown them to him. Take my advice and stop your threats. If he saw the note you gave me with the wrong address and the letter from Lev Feinberg you hid he would surely rework the contract in a way that would punish you and your mother. I wouldn't want to do that to your *mother!*"

Pinhas opened his mouth, preparing to come back with a retort. Realizing his position, he suddenly stopped, closed his mouth, and, with a look of surrender, turned and walked away.

Solomon's health continued to deteriorate over the coming months, but he was filled with a powerful zeal to help Izzy learn the intricacies of the fur business. His doctor had advised him that the only way he might lengthen his life was if he spent much of his time resting at home. But that life was no life at all to Solomon Goldman.

Late on the night following the family meeting he sat down at his desk and wrote a list of what he wanted to achieve before he died:

1. Teach Izzy enough about the business so that I feel sure he will succeed and the business will survive.

2. Take care of my sister's and nephew's financial needs.

3. Be able to assure my faithful workers they will continue to have employment.

4. Set aside money for Oheb Zedek synagogue and for the Hebrew Immigrant Aid Society to be donated after my death.

Solomon, despite his failing health, continued to work at one thing or another to help the business every day; he would meet with and advise Izzy nearly every day. On days when he had enough strength he walked through the fur shop, inspecting the work being done.

During this period Izzy was working long hours and came home exhausted every night. It was the kind of exhaustion that was easy to bear. He could see a time when his hard work would be handsomely rewarded.

Chapter 35

Izzy Asks for Advice

Life continued pretty much the same until Izzy received a letter from Dorothy saying she and Morris were on their way to Cleveland and would arrive in about a month. She explained that her older brother would not be coming. He was married, had a new baby, and was employed by his new father-in-law.

As the time grew shorter Izzy found himself thinking about Dorothy constantly. Once again, he was remembering how after he had met and spent time with her in London he had promised himself he would marry that girl someday. He had to admit, though, that the thought was a foolish one at the time. After all, she was just a child of twelve and he was a man of eighteen. She lived in London and he was on his way to America. Would her parents approve? Would she want to marry him? When he first met her she was so pretty, clever, and friendly. Surely some other young men would be very interested in her. And now, against all those odds, she would be coming to Cleveland.

Late at night, Izzy, lying in bed, would close his eyes and try to imagine what Dorothy might look like now. He saw that flaming red hair of hers and captivating smile. He remembered the sound of her voice and wondered how it might sound now. And some nights he would dream about his love-making with Mathilda, but Mathilda would suddenly turn into what he imagined Dorothy looked like now.

Somehow, in some part of his soul, he felt this was all meant to be— that Dorothy was destined to be his bride. But there were questions and issues to be resolved. He had grown up in a world where marriages were arranged by *shadchuns* (marriage brokers) and required the consent of the father. What could be done with Dorothy's parents dead and his so far away?

Israel, who out of respect for his employer always addressed him as Mr. Goldman, spoke to him about the subject one day. He approached it this way.

"Mr. Goldman, I have a friend who needs some advice. He wants to marry a girl, but her parents are dead and his parents are in the old country. The girl has two brothers. Does he need to go through a shadchun or can he ask her brothers for permission to marry her?"

Solomon, who liked to think that when he was asked for advice, he could offer it with the wisdom of the king who was his namesake, first asked, "Is he sure the girl wants to marry him?"

"Well, to tell the truth, he doesn't know for sure, but he is very hopeful."

"This friend lives in America?"

"Yes, he does."

"I know how it was in Poland. Many people still do it that way because that is all they know. But now, here in America, things such as this can be different. We have more freedom, so yes, if your friend's girl wants to marry him he should be able to do so. But in this case, since her parents are gone, it would be wise for him to ask permission from her oldest brother."

"Thank you, Mr. Goldman. I'll tell my friend what you told me. He will be pleased with the advice you offered."

Solomon Goldman smiled broadly, a knowing smile, and said, "Oh, I suspect your friend already has the advice."

Chapter 36

Dorothy Seeks Advice

Dorothy Greenbaum was frantically working at readying herself and her brother Morris for their journey to America. Time was running out.

She was growing more excited every day. But the excitement wasn't merely about the trip. It was mostly about seeing Israel Singer again now that she was a grown-up woman of sixteen. She was uncertain and confused about her feelings and needed to talk to someone about them. With her parents gone she thought of the close friends of her family, Mr. and Mrs. Jacob Usher Singer, Israel's uncle and aunt. She visited them and asked if she could talk to Mrs. Singer alone. This was woman talk.

"So, what's on your mind, Dorothy? You look troubled."

"As you know, we're going to America next week. Your nephew Israel will be finding us a place to live."

"Yes, I know. What is the problem?"

"Ever since Israel visited here on his way to America I have been thinking about him. We have been writing letters and they have been getting more personal all the time. Do you know what I mean?"

"No, exactly what do you mean?"

"Well, you see, even though we have been so far away, we have drawn closer together."

"Is that bad?"

"No, but what will happen when we see each other? Do you think he will like me? I'm so skinny."

"Skinny, schminny! You're a beautiful girl. Not only that, but you are smart. And I remember how proud your mother was of your cooking and baking."

"Do you really think he will like me?"

"You are hoping he will want to marry you...yes?"

Dorothy blushed, looked away for a moment, and wrung her hands.

"Yes, but what will happen if he doesn't want to marry me? I don't know what I'll do."

"Dorothy, my darling, he would be a fool if he didn't want to marry you. And I don't think my nephew is a fool."

"Alright, so if he does want to marry me, what do I do? I don't know anything about how to be a good wife."

"Dorothy, did your mother talk to you about what happens on your wedding night and about how babies are made?"

"Yes…and I remember how surprised I was!"

"Well, if you know that and how to cook and clean, you will figure all the rest out just like all the rest of us."

Dorothy sat quietly for a moment and thought about what she had heard, then she said, "Thank you. I feel better now."

Chapter 37

Israel Worries

Israel grew more excited each day as he anticipated the arrival of Dorothy and her brother. But he was also very worried. He kept visualizing them as they would be confronting all of the problems and challenges he had faced. After all, he was a grown-up man of eighteen when he set off for America. Dorothy was just sixteen and Morris was two years younger. He thought about them crossing the endless ocean. He worried about them as he recalled the stress of passing through Ellis Island. He prayed they would both pass the physical examination and not have to (God forbid!) be sent back to England. He feared for their safety when they had to pass through the gauntlet of scoundrels they would encounter when they reached New York. He even worried they might somehow be seduced by the lure of New York's excitement and decide to stay there. He wondered how they would feel about Cleveland once they arrived and saw what it looked like.

Israel had incredibly powerful memories of the beautiful red-haired girl who at the age of twelve had stolen his heart. Dorothy had sent him a photo taken when she was fifteen. In it her face appeared to be even more beautiful and her figure...well, she already had the body of a grown woman!

But now Israel had good reason to worry about Dorothy and Morris. It was three days past the day they were supposed to arrive in Cleveland. He couldn't help thinking about all the terrible things that might have happened to them. As he had begun to do often when he had a problem, Israel went to Solomon Goldman's home to seek counsel and advice from his mentor. Solomon assured him that three days late was not unusual and tried to calm his young protégé.

Solomon asked, "So tell me more about this Dorothy. I have heard you speak of her often and can't wait to meet her."

"Mr. Goldman, she is the most beautiful, wonderful girl. But not only that, she is also very smart. Have I shown you her picture?"

"Israel. You have shown it to me many times and I can see why you feel the way you do about her. So, what's going to happen when she gets here? And stop worrying so much. She will get here soon. You'll see."

"What do you mean what will happen? I have found a home for her and her brother. They have some money with them and I'll help them out until they can find work."

"Israel, my son, it's about time for you to think about getting married and raising a family. I don't think we are going to need a *Shadchun* for you. You say this Dorothy is sixteen? She looks like the right wife for you. I have a feeling this was all meant to be. I only pray I will live long enough to see you married. Now boychik, go back to work and let me know when your bride-to-be arrives."

Chapter 38

The Requirements

It was now their third day in Cleveland, Ohio. Morris and Dorothy were still physically exhausted after their long and harrowing journey. But they were filled with the optimistic excitement of youth, and that energized them as they took in their new surroundings and met new people. Earlier that day Izzy had taken them to the fur shop and introduced them to Solomon Goldman and all the workers.

When they got back to the house where the brother and sister would be renting rooms, Morris, sensing that Izzy and Dorothy wanted to be alone, said, "I'm going to go exploring. I'll see you later."

Dorothy chided, "Don't get lost like you did in New York, Morris."

"Don't worry. Cleveland looks like it's a lot easier to get around in." With that, he turned, grinned at the couple, and was out the door.

Izzy said, "It's a beautiful day. Let's go out on the porch and sit on the swing."

They sat in silence, gently swinging for a few minutes.

Finally, Izzy, who was hoping to steer the conversation in a matrimonial direction, said, "Dorothy, I wonder if you have any idea about how much I have been looking forward to your coming here. It's all I have been thinking about for months. So tell me, now that you are here, what do you want to do?"

"Well, Israel (she still couldn't get herself to call him Izzy), I'll be honest, as I have always been with you. I think my goal should be to find a good husband."

The candidness of her response surprised and encouraged Izzy. "Tell me, Dorothy, what kind of a husband do you want?"

"Israel, I've thought a lot about that and I think I know exactly what I'm looking for in a husband. In fact, in my mind I have a list of requirements all figured out."

"Dorothy, if it's okay with you I'd like to write them down. Then if I see someone who meets those requirements I can introduce him to you. I always have my pencil and pieces of paper with me, so if think of something I need for the business I can write it down. Now, go ahead....."

"I've always pictured a man that is not too tall, only slightly taller than me."

"You mean around my height?"

"Yes, exactly."

Izzy wrote:

1. My height.

"I prefer brown hair, neatly combed, something like yours."

2. My hair.

"Of course, he must be from a good Jewish family."

Izzy liked where the conversation was going and replied, "You mean from a family where the man's father is a rabbi or a sofer?"

"Oh, yes, that would be perfect!"

3. My family.

"He should be smart in business so he could provide for his family and make enough to afford giving to charity."

"You mean like a man who runs a clothing or fur business?"

"Yes. One of those would be just right."

4. My business.

"He should be kind, gentle, and generous."

"What about a man who helped a woman and her brother come to America?"

Dorothy smiled broadly and declared, "Where could I possibly find such a man?"

Izzy, enjoying the game, made a show of looking at his list. Then he declared, "I think I know just such a person. But what about love? Would you feel you and the man you require could learn to love each other?"

"Oh, that's not an issue. I've been in love with that man since the first day I met him. But I don't know if he feels the same way about me, because up until this moment, he never said so."

Izzy nervously reached for Dorothy's hand, and having heard about the often observed tradition, slipped down to the floor on one knee and said, "Dorothy Greenbaum, I have met all of your requirements for a husband, I love you, and I have wanted to marry ever since I looked at your beautiful face. Will you marry me?"

"Of course I'll marry you, Israel. Now get up off your knee and kiss me."

Chapter 39

Three Days Before the Wedding

It was Thursday, September 5, 1910 and a beautiful fall day in Cleveland. The leaves on the sycamore trees were just beginning to turn many shades of gold. Izzy had left the fur shop a little early. There was much to do to get ready for the wedding on Sunday and he also wanted to visit Dorothy.

After his uncle had made the arrangement to sell his business to Izzy Singer, Pinhas Slobodnik began drinking heavily. His preferred libation was one hundred proof bourbon. He had also become a heavy smoker, going through a pack of Murad Turkish cigarettes every day or two. Although he came to work at the fur shop every day at the insistence of his mother, there was little he was able to do well, so Izzy seldom asked Pinhas to do anything. Sometimes he came to work drunk or hungover. On his particularly bad days Pinhas would sneak into a storage room in the basement of the building, pile up scrap fur pieces on the floor, and take a nap. There was really no need for him to sneak into his den. Everyone in the shop was onto his antics.

Pinhas had lost his self-respect and become an embarrassment to his mother and uncle, both of whom felt powerless to effect any change in him. They tried sending him to some cousins in Columbus. Perhaps getting him away from the fur shop and its reminder of his failure might help him move into a better a frame of mind. But Pinhas refused to go. He feared the cousins wouldn't put up with his drinking and smoking.

After awakening from his nap this Thursday, he pulled a cigarette out of the orange box, struck a match with the expertise of a chain smoker, and lit the cigarette. Being in the basement room, Pinhas was unaware that the shop was closed. Everyone had gone home.

Solomon Goldman, having not gone to the shop since Monday because of his weakening heart, was feeling better after having rested. Having concerns about a new employee and how sales were going, he sent a note to Israel asking him to meet him at the shop at seven that evening. With his dark oak cane in hand Solomon walked the two blocks to the shop.

Pinhas, after finishing his smoke, carelessly dropped the butt onto the pile of fur scraps, left the shop by the back door, and staggered home. Somewhere in the back of his fog-clouded brain there was a hint of the idea that his cigarette butt might have not been entirely extinguished.

At first, the idea he might have burned the building down put a smile on his face. "What a great way to get revenge on that damn Izzy!" But then he started to feel stabs of remorse and regret as he remembered that if the shop burned down he and his mother would lose their income.

Pinhas then convinced himself there was nothing to worry about. He was sure the cigarette butt was out.

At two minutes before seven, Solomon unlocked the front door of the shop. He was on his way to his office when suddenly he smelled smoke.

Chapter 40

Two Letters

September 2, 1910

Dear Mama and Papa,

I have much to tell you. You remember I wrote you about how the friends of Uncle Jacob, the Greenbaums in London, died and left their children as orphans? I have been writing to their daughter Dorothy ever since we met when I was in London. Now they have come to Cleveland. I hope you won't be upset when I tell you I made up my mind to marry Dorothy. She is a wonderful girl from a fine family. Someday you will meet her and I know you will love her as I do.

She and her younger brother Morris bravely made the long trip to America. I was worried about them when they were traveling to America. When they were three days late in getting here I went crazy with worry. They had gotten lost and went on to a city called Detroit. But some very kind people helped them and they found their way to Cleveland. I found a nice place for them to live.

My job is going well. Mr. Goldman has been kind to me. He is old and sick and cannot run his business anymore. He trusted me as a worker so much, he made arrangements for me to buy his business over a period of several years. I am in charge of the fur shop and I am making a good living. I'm making such a good living, I know I am ready to get married and have a family.

I will be marrying Dorothy Greenbaum this coming weekend. I so wish you could be here for the celebration. We will be married under a Chupah by Rabbi Gross at Oheb Zedek. I have made many friends who will be coming to the wedding. We will even have a klezmer band of musicians who all came here from Russia and Poland. I am very happy and feel like my move to America was the most wonderful thing that ever happened to me.

Someday I will make my dream come true and help all of you come to America.

Shalom from your loving son,

Israel

November 14, 1910

Dear Israel,

Mazel tov on your wedding. We got a letter from Jacob and he told us what a wonderful new daughter-in-law we have. He was thrilled to learn that you married Dorothy. We felt much better about your wedding after we heard from Jacob. We are very proud of you and what you have done in America. Avrum Binstock has been telling everyone about your success. He told us that you have already paid him back the money he gave you to make the trip.

Our apartment is getting very crowded now that we have five children. I know you would love to see your new sister Perl. She is such a beautiful baby. I am working on a new Torah for the Synagogue in Sokolow. We are beginning to worry about Herschel. He is fifteen and soon will be old enough to be conscripted into the army. You have written about wanting to help the family come to America. I hope you can help Herschel first when the time comes.

Life is much the same as it was when you were here. But we are always hearing about pogroms in Russia and also many people have died because of that terrible disease cholera. We hear there are no pogroms in America. Are there bad diseases where you live? We hope not. Please take care of your health. We miss you very much. We pray for the day when our whole family will be together again.

Shalom, L'hitraot (Until we meet again),

Chaim Zynger

Chapter 41

Emergency

After work, Izzy rushed around from place to place, first to Oheb Zedek synagogue to see Rabbi Gross about the wedding ceremony, then to Harry Cole, the photographer for wedding photos. His next stop was to see Benny Brussel, the leader of the Klezmer band.

With Dorothy setting up house with him, Izzy had to find a place for her brother Morris to live. He called on his old landlady/lover Mathilda Garson for advice. He hadn't seen her for some time, and although they were no longer lovers he knew they would always be friends. And of course, he had invited her to his wedding.

After he told her about Morris, she said, "Izzy, my darling, you came to the right place to ask for help. It just so happens that I know this couple, the Brauns, Laurence and Natalie. They have a big house with lots of room. All their boys grew up and moved out. I also happen to know they could use a few extra dollars from a boarder. Tell me, Izzy, is this Morris skinny?" Before Izzy could answer, she continued, "A few months eating Natalie's cooking and don't worry, he won't be skinny anymore." Izzy wrote down the address of the Braun home. He thanked Mathilda, and said, "Good-bye, I'll see you and your husband at the wedding." She gave him a hug and then a peck on the cheek.

Izzy pulled out the gold pocket watch Solomon had given to him for his twenty-second birthday. The time was six twenty. He wanted to get back to the shop on time for his seven o'clock appointment with Solomon. But now it was time to visit Dorothy. He trotted to the house where she and Morris were living. They had just finished dinner and were cleaning the dishes when Izzy rang the doorbell.

Dorothy seemed a little flustered when she saw Izzy. She didn't know he was coming and always wanted to look her best for him. Her red hair needed brushing and she was wearing a very plain house dress.

But none of that mattered to Izzy. He was so filled with awe and wonder as he constantly thought about how he met this beautiful girl, dreamed of marrying her someday, and now it was all, unbelievably, coming true.

They sat on the sofa in the living room and Izzy filled Dorothy in on all of the arrangements that had been made. She was impressed and pleased to see how well her husband to-be handled everything. He then told Morris about the Brauns and promised to make arrangements to take him to meet them as soon as he could.

It was now six forty-two and Izzy had just enough time to reach the shop by seven if he hurried. He started out at a trot, which soon turned into a sprint. When he reached the front door of the shop he was surprised to find the door open and unlocked. It wasn't like Solomon to leave the door open.

He looked for Solomon. The smell of smoke reached him. He heard a sound from the basement.

Solomon had determined that the smoke was wafting up from a room in the basement. Climbing down stairs was difficult for him. He struggled taking each step, frustrated that he couldn't move more quickly. When he reached the bottom, he saw where the smoke was coming from. A thick, choking cloud of pungent black smoke enveloped him.

He coughed violently. That was the sound Izzy heard. Izzy flew down the stairs, but he couldn't see clearly. Smoke was pouring out of the room where Pinhas often went to hide and sleep. He shouted, "Pinhas, are you there?"

A figure emerged from the cloud of smoke. It was Solomon Goldman. Izzy ran to him and helped him up the stairs and out of the building. Then he frantically grabbed buckets, filled them with water, took a deep breath, and charged into the smoke-filled room, half expecting to see Pinhas lying on the floor.

No one was in the room. The smoke was flowing from smoldering scraps of fur on the floor. Gradually, as Izzy soaked the furs with water, the smoke subsided. In half an hour everything on the basement floor was soaked and the fire was completely out.

With the fire out, Izzy turned his attention to helping his mentor. He had recently convinced Solomon to install that new invention called the telephone in the shop. He remembered it when he fought the fire, but felt it would take too long to call the fire department and wait for them to get there. But now, with Solomon coughing violently and gasping for breath, he phoned Dr. Gittleson.

The doctor drove a Ford model T and arrived quickly. Solomon's coughing finally stopped but he turned very pale and began to collapse; Izzy had eased him down on the soft grass in front of the building. Dr. Gittleson examined Solomon and asked Izzy to help get him into his car. As the doctor drove to Saint Ann's Hospital, Izzy asked him if Solomon was going to be okay. He only shook his head and said, "I don't know."

Chapter 42

Two Women Helpers

With the wedding approaching, there was much to do. Although Dorothy was smart and clever beyond her years, she would have felt overwhelmed if it were not for the two women who stepped in to help her. The first was Mathilda Garson, Izzy's former lover/landlady, now happily married and secure. When she heard about Izzy's forthcoming wedding to the young girl who had recently so tragically lost both her parents, her heart went out to Dorothy and Izzy. She volunteered to help in any way she could.

Mathilda offering to help was not surprising. What was surprising was Hannah Slobodnik offering to help as well. Hannah was at first embittered by the arrangement her brother had made with Izzy. But as time passed she came to realize the wisdom of her brother's decision. Hannah had finally come to terms with the flaws in her son's character. She understood how Izzy running the business would be the best way to ensure her future security. And, in fact, she had grown fond of Izzy, much to her son's displeasure. When Hannah met the charming young Dorothy and learned of the forthcoming marriage she was motivated to offer her help to the soon-to-be bride. She had never had a daughter of her own…this would be the next best thing.

And so, the two women helped Dorothy choose a wedding dress and all the needed accessories. They showed her where to get this and that and even arranged a bridal shower. Because Dorothy knew so few people, most of the gifts came from the two women.

Dorothy and Izzy

Chapter 43

The Wedding Day

On the morning of the wedding, Solomon Goldman was lying in his bed at Saint Ann's Hospital, seriously ill. His eyes opened slowly. He thought, "Where am I?"

It took a few moments to remember what had happened to him. Raising his head brought on violent coughing. Hearing his cough, the nurse came into his room with a bottle of cough syrup with laudanum. She greeted him cheerily, gave him a teaspoon of the bitter-tasting opium and alcohol-laced drug, and took his pulse.

Speaking softly and hoarsely, Solomon asked, "What day is this? Is it Sunday?"

When she said yes, he thought, "Today is the wedding! I must get up!"

He tried to get out of bed. The nurse shouted, "No, Mr. Goldman, you must not do that!"

Solomon soon realized he was too weak and dizzy to get up. Still in a disoriented state of mind, he tried to think of what he could do about the wedding he had so looked forward to attending. When his mind cleared he called the nurse and asked her to write a message and to please telephone Izzy and read it to him. It read, "I'm so sorry I won't be able to come to your wedding. I wish you and Dorothy a wonderful lifetime of happiness together."

The nurse phoned Izzy. After she read the brief message to him Izzy inquired about Solomon's condition. She replied, "Mr. Goldman's condition is very serious. Perhaps I shouldn't tell you this, but I don't think his chances are very good." When Izzy received that message, he knew that no matter how busy he was on this, his wedding day, he must see Solomon.

He rushed to Dorothy's house and told her they had to go to the hospital. Izzy had recently learned to drive and owned a Royal Model G car, manufactured in Cleveland. They drove to the hospital and on the way picked up Solomon's sister Hannah. When Izzy inquired about her son Pinhas, she shook her head and said, "I don't know where he is, Izzy. I'm very worried about him. I haven't seen him for two days."

Izzy, Dorothy, and Hannah entered Solomon's hospital room. He was asleep. They stood quietly near his bed for several minutes. There were three other patients in the room, the beds separated by white curtains. When Hannah noticed her brother's pale color she was shocked and began sobbing. She had seen the look of impending death many times before and now saw it in her own brother.

Hannah's sobbing woke Solomon. When he saw Izzy and Dorothy approach his bed, he summoned all his strength and will power. Smiling weakly, in a barely audible raspy voice, he uttered, "What are you doing here with this sick old man? This is your wedding day. This is not the place for you to be. Go, get married. Have a beautiful wedding and a beautiful long life together. Don't worry about me. The doctor is taking good care of me."

Taking Solomon's hand in his and fighting back tears, Izzy said, "Mr. Goldman, we were very worried about you and just couldn't go to the wedding without visiting you first. None of this would have been possible without your kindness and generosity. Now please rest and get better and we'll tell you all about the wedding after we get back from Niagara Falls." With that said, Dorothy kissed Solomon on the cheek, followed by Hannah, who was still sobbing.

Izzy drove both women to Dorothy's home, where Mathilda Garson was waiting to help the bride prepare for the wedding. Mathilda had also made arrangements to take the bride to the synagogue. Two hours later everyone had gathered at Oheb Zedek for the ceremony.

Having heard what Hannah said about Pinhas being missing, Izzy was troubled. He called Sam and Oscar over to him. They were two of his shop workers who were close friends and confidants.

Speaking in a confidential voice he said, "Pinhas is the one who caused the fire in the shop. He hasn't been seen for two days. I don't know what is going on with him, but I'm worried he might show up drunk at the wedding. Will you two please keep a lookout for him?"

Sam answered, "Sure Izzy, we'll take care of Pinhas. Don't you worry."

The synagogue was prepared for the wedding with the *chuppah* (wedding canopy) made up of a very large, ornate *talit* (prayer shawl) Dorothy had given to Izzy as a gift. It was attached to four poles set on the *bimah* (platform) in front of the *aron ha kodesh* (cabinet that houses the Torah). Beautiful floral arrangements decorated the bimah, their fragrance floating through the room. The first order of business before the wedding ceremony was the signing of the *ketuba* (marriage contract) by the bride and groom and two witnesses.

As required, Dorothy had been to the *mikveh* (ritual bathhouse). Following an ancient orthodox tradition called, in Yiddish, *badeken die kallah*[7],

---

[7] Derived from the biblical story of Jacob, who worked for seven years to marry Rachel, only to discover her father had substituted Leah, under heavy veiling.

the groom was escorted by the rabbi, the cantor, and the male guests to where the bride Dorothy was waiting, her face uncovered. After being viewed by Izzy, he covered her face with the veil. The assembled guests then recited the blessing that was pronounced over the Matriarch Rebecca: "Our sister, may you become the mother of thousands, of tens of thousands" (Genesis 24:60).

The wedding ceremony began. Izzy, accompanied by two friends holding lighted candles, was led down the aisle to the chuppah, with music provided by the cantor and a choir of men and boys. Next, Dorothy was led down the aisle by Hannah and Mathilda, also carrying lighted candles. Dorothy, who had seen the custom before at several weddings, circled Izzy seven times. Then she took her place under the chuppah at Izzy's right side. The rabbi recited the two benedictions over a cup of wine, which was then given to the bride and groom to drink. Next, Izzy placed the wedding ring on Dorothy's finger as he declared in Hebrew, "Hereby you are consecrated to me with this ring, in accordance with the laws of Moses and Israel."

Next came the reading of the Ketubah, setting forth the mutual obligations of the newlyweds. Following that and six more blessings recited by the rabbi, a glass was placed on the floor. With one mighty stomp by Izzy it was shattered, followed by shouts of "Mazel tov!" The happy couple came back down the aisle to the cheers of all. Everyone moved to the social hall, where generous portions of food and drink were served. Klezmer music was provided by a group of players on mandolin, violin, clarinet, piano, string bass, and drums.

Sam and Oscar were relieved to note that Pinhas had not shown up during the ceremony, but were still vigilant. After ten minutes of celebration, Pinhas, drunk and staggering, appeared at the door of the social hall. Oscar called to Sam. They met Pinhas at the door, each taking one arm, turned him around, and marched him to Oscar's car.

Pinhas struggled but was overpowered. He was put into the back seat of the car. Sam turned to Oscar and said, "Where should we take him?"

Oscar smiled and whispered in Sam's ear, "Some place where it will take him a long time to get back. How about way out on Euclid Avenue in East Cleveland?"

At one point during the reception Izzy looked around and noticed that Sam and Oscar were missing. He knew they must have seen Pinhas trying to come to the wedding. Izzy was relieved later when he saw them come back into the hall. The three men got together and drank a toast of a shot of whiskey. Izzy and Dorothy said their good-byes and prepared to leave the hall. Their suitcases loaded in Sam's car, they waved good-bye to everyone and Sam drove them to the train station, where they were bound for Buffalo and Niagara Falls.

Meanwhile, Pinhas had found himself one hundred forty blocks from

Oheb Zedek. He was still determined to get to the wedding. By the time he reached Oheb Zedek, walking several blocks and taking two street cars, no one was left at the synagogue but the cleaners. Pinhas was, by that time, sober. It was now dark and had grown cold. As he stood alone, shivering in the dark on the steps of the synagogue, he thought about all that had happened during the past few days...how he had gotten drunk and caused the fire, how his uncle had to be rushed to the hospital because of his carelessness and might now be dying. And then he was kicked out of the wedding.

His first tendency was to blame all his problems on Izzy. He was struggling to resist the idea that he himself was to blame. Yet, in his gut he knew that to be the truth. The question was, could he live with that knowledge?

Chapter 44

After the Honeymoon

When Izzy and Dorothy got off the train home, Sam and Oscar were there to greet them and help with the luggage of the young honeymooners. On their way home Dorothy was bubbling over with tales about the spectacular beauty of Niagara Falls. Then Izzy turned to Sam and asked, "How is Mr. Goldman?"

The silence from the two men told Izzy more than words. Finally, Oscar said, "Izzy, he didn't suffer long. He died in his sleep two nights ago. The funeral was yesterday. I'm sorry we couldn't wait for you to get back."

Izzy, stunned by the news, just sat quietly for several minutes. Then he said, "Take us to where he was buried. We just want to pay our respects."

During the next six days Dorothy, Izzy, and most of the workers in the shop, as well as Solomon Goldman's friends, sat *shiva* (a gathering of the mourners for seven days) every evening at Hannah's home. A very quiet and sober Pinhas was there every evening. At the end of the week he and Hannah came to see Izzy.

They sat down in the office that had been Solomon's and was now Izzy's. Hannah began, "Pinhas has something to say to you, don't you?"

Pinhas sat quietly and uncomfortably, then finally said, "I'm going to live with my uncle in Columbus. I'm leaving tomorrow."

Glowering at him, Hannah said, "Yes, Pinhas, and what else did you want to say?"

"Izzy, I'm sorry…sorry about everything. I'm especially sorry about the fire. I had too much to drink. Now I'm going away."

With that said, he looked at his mother. Hannah, who wept easily, had her handkerchief at the ready. Finally she looked at Pinhas and nodded her approval.

Izzy thought about what he would say. He was very angry with Pinhas and fighting to control his temper. He studied Pinhas, who was for the first time actually looking sincerely contrite. And then he looked at Hannah, who was now sobbing uncontrollably.

Izzy thought, "For Hannah's sake, I will try to make the situation better."

"I think that was an apology, Pinhas. If it was, I accept it, and I hope you do well in Columbus with your uncle. Now, if you will both excuse me, I have a fur shop to run."

The Solomon Goldman Company stayed closed for the first three days. Then Izzy got in touch with all the workers. When they met in the shop he assured them they would all be keeping their jobs as long as everyone worked hard. Then he pledged to do everything he could to make sure the business would not only continue, but he also predicted it would grow in the coming years. It was with heavy hearts but a sense of determination that everyone went back to work.

Chapter 45

Life Moves On

Our story moves on through the years. Izzy was managing the fur shop admirably during this time, as he was settling into married life. In October of 1911 the couple's first child, Lillian Rose, was born.

During that time Izzy became aware of the storm clouds of war gathering in Europe. He was deeply concerned about the safety of his family back in Poland, and especially about his brother Herschel, who was approaching an age when he would likely be subject to the dreaded conscription into the Polish army.

Izzy began a correspondence with Herschel, to encourage his younger brother to join him in America and help him make enough money to bring the rest of the family to America. Izzy was able to send some money, but not enough to pay for the whole trip. He was still struggling to make the business succeed and now had the extra burden of a growing family.

Like Izzy before him, Herschel was aided by his uncle Avrum Binstock, who helped him with both encouragement and money to make the trip. Fortunately, Herschel was able to leave Poland for America in 1914, just prior to the beginning of World War I. Herschel Zynger, who became Harry Singer in America, immediately became a valuable worker in the fur shop and his management talent soon became apparent.

The war in Europe continued to rage on, preventing any possibility of bringing the Zynger family to America, but both brothers, Izzy and Herschel, began laying the groundwork for their big project. In the meantime, both the fur shop and Izzy's family were growing. Dorothy, now more commonly called Dora, gave birth to Gertrude (Kay) in April of 1916 and their third daughter, Shirley Betty, was born in March of 1920, on her mother's twenty-sixth birthday.

In the meantime, as the war devastated Europe, in Losice the Germans had commandeered the second-floor three-room apartment of the Zynger family. Chaim, Dina, and their five children moved into one of the two smaller apartments on the ground floor. (The building had been given to Chaim by his father, so they lived rent-free and derived some income renting out the other units.)

During the war, life changed drastically. Thinking about how circumstances would change a scant twenty years later, it is surprising to learn that the Germans treated the Zynger family well, even giving them food from time to time. Actually, the Bolsheviks (Russians) were more feared than the Germans.

There was fighting in and around Losice and nearby Sokolow. At times the family had to hide in nearby fields because of the fighting. Daughter Pearl recalled hiding in the cellar one frightening night when the town's lone drugstore was burned to the ground. But the family survived, despite terror, hunger, and shortages of all kinds. After the war, they received money from their two American sons and Chaim's brother Usher, who had moved to South Africa.

By 1918 Izzy's family had moved to a new Jewish neighborhood in Cleveland, along East 105th Street: the first floor of a spacious two-story, two-family home on Yale Avenue. It was typical of the homes in the area in that it had a full basement and an attic. Sycamore trees provided shade in the hot summers and lilac bushes bloomed in many yards.

Many new Jewish families arrived in Cleveland from Europe after the war, including the Friedmans from the shtetl Sokolow, located near Losice. The four Friedman children included Norman, Morton, Alvin, and Frieda. Harry married Frieda Friedman in Cleveland in 1921.

By 1921 Izzy and Harry had filled out the necessary papers and had gathered together enough money to bring the rest of the family to America. And now we begin the Zynger family saga....

Part 3:
The Zynger
Family Saga

Chapter 46

The Decision

Chaim was bent over his work, struggling to concentrate but knowing he must soon stop his work and prepare for Shabbos. It was Friday and he had to go to the *mikvah*, the ritual bathhouse, and cleanse himself, and then put on clean clothes in order to greet the holiest day of the week properly as a devout Jew. As a sofer, a scribe of Torahs, he was expected to live an exemplary orthodox Jewish life in every respect.

There was a serious question he had been struggling with for several weeks. The decision couldn't be delayed any longer. He had been working on this Torah for nearly a year and now he had, at last, reached the final section of *Dvorim* (Deuteronomy).

"Moses went up from the steppes of Moab to Mount Nebo, to the summit of Pisgah, opposite Jericho, and the lord showed him the whole land...."

Gazing at these words and then carefully inscribing them on the calfskin before him made him think about the land he and his ancestors had lived in for generations, and whether the new land his sons wanted him to come to, like Abraham and the ancient Israelites, would be the promised land for him and his progeny.

Chaim had told Dina, his wife, his four daughters, Shayna Chaya, Sura Basha, Perl, and Menicha, and Natan, the one son who still lived with the family, that he couldn't do anything until this Torah was completed to his satisfaction. He was proud to know that it would soon sit majestically in the splendid Ark of one of Warsaw's great synagogues. He felt this was his very best Torah and had a deep sense of pride in what he had, with God's help, been able to do.

Torahs must, in every way, be perfect. No mistakes in the text are allowed, even though it is a long and complicated task to write the entire Five Books of Moses in Hebrew. It must be done entirely by hand, with a quill from a turkey or goose feather, using kosher ink made, incredibly, from the crushed outer bark of a wasp's nest. The eighty parchment pages must be made from a calf that has been killed for food. Although he had never counted them, he would have been awed to learn that each Torah he had penned contained 304,805 letters, no more, no less.

Chaim Zynger was a man of average height for the time, a little over five feet four inches. Yet he appeared taller, perhaps because of his erect posture, thin face, and long, narrow beard. He had the piercing eyes of a man who had spent a lifetime reading and writing the holiest of manuscripts. His voice was soft but authoritative and evoked the respect one has for a wise man. He could speak Polish, but preferred and almost exclusively spoke Yiddish, the thousand-year-old language of the Jewish people that had its roots in Hebrew, Aramaic, Slavonic, and German. Just as music is an international language among musicians all over the world, Yiddish was a language that crossed many borders and made it possible for Jews from different countries to converse with one another.

Now that Chaim was nearly done with writing his twentieth Torah, he had to decide on a course of action that he knew would change the lives of everyone in his family for generations to come. He had discussed the matter with Dina, his rabbi, his friends, and other family members. Knowing the final decision was his and his alone weighed heavily upon him.

Fathering three fine sons should have been a great blessing, but in those times in that land, it could also be a source of heartbreak, and that is why the decision had to be made. All young men were subject to conscription into the Polish army for a period of twenty years. It was well known that the Polish army was institutionally anti-Semitic. Many Jewish men, often assigned to jobs like pulling the cannons, did not survive to return to their families. This was common knowledge in their shtetl, Losice, and other villages throughout the country. That is why Chaim and Dina, with heavy hearts and copious weeping, had sent their two eldest sons, first Israel in 1906 and then Herschel in 1914, to America.

And now those sons had sent letters begging their father to bring the whole family to America. Chaim hesitated for many reasons. He was, after all, a revered member of his Jewish community. His family, unlike many others, was not impoverished. They owned a small apartment house in which they lived rent-free. Losice had been their family home for generations. Chaim was also worried that they would not be able to live an orthodox Jewish life in the place called Cleveland, where their sons had settled. When learning of this last concern, Israel arranged to have a Cleveland rabbi write a letter to Chaim, assuring him that he could indeed keep a kosher home and live an orthodox religious life in Cleveland.

At first Chaim offered to send only their two eldest daughters, Shayna Chaya and Sura Basha, but Israel and Herschel stood firm, writing "all or none." So, he had to decide.

Chapter 47

Dina

Sometime around 1887, in the village of Losice, east of Warsaw, Poland, Chaim sofer Zynger, son of Beryl and Shayna Chaya Zynger, married Dina, daughter of Mendel and Sura Basha Oxengoren. Beginning in 1888 and over the next twenty-five years, Dina gave birth to eight children. First there were four sons and then four daughters. The firstborn son only lived to the age of ten, when an ear infection forced the family to seek help from a doctor in Warsaw, where the boy died.

Dina was thinking about her life, about her two sons in America, and worrying about her youngest son, Natan, as she walked in the hot summer sun. Her two older daughters, Shayna Chaya and Sura Basha, were tagging along behind her, carrying empty baskets. She was heading for the farm of Mr. Charkoff, one of the few Jewish farmers in the area. Mr. Charkoff had chickens and geese and he grew potatoes, turnips, and the biggest cabbages and beets she had ever seen. When they saw her coming, the farmer and his wife came out of their house and greeted her, saying, "Shalom, Dina, how is the sofer and what are the names of your beautiful daughters?" As they were greeting her, the farmer went to his well and drew out a large ladle of cool water, which he offered to Dina and the girls. They thanked him before they gulped down the water and politely asked for more, to wash the dust of the road off of their hands and faces.

"Shalom," Dina replied, and then, after introducing her daughters, she asked about the health of the Charkoff family members.

Shlomo Charkoff laughed and said, "We have just been blessed with our first grandson. He will be named Yitzchak and you are invited to the *Pidyon Haben*[8] at the end of the month. We will have a fine celebration. Come and bring your children, please."

"Mazel tov," Dina said. "How exciting. You are so kind to invite the whole family. I don't know if Chaim can come. He is very busy finishing the writing of a Torah that must be ready by the end of the month, but we will

---

[8] Translated as "redeeming the son," the Pidyon Haben is a ceremony whereby the firstborn child is redeemed from priestly obligations by the Kohen of the synagogue, with a small payment.

all try to come to share your joy."

Just then, Shlomo's tall slender son, Yitzhak, came in from the forest, where he had been cutting wood. He was perspiring heavily as he headed to the well for a drink, but stopped and smiled when he saw the two young Zynger girls.

"Dina, this is our son Yitzhak," Shlomo said. Yitzhak bowed his head as he was introduced. And then, as he turned toward the girls, his father said, "Moshe, these are Mrs. Zynger's daughters, Shayna and Sura Basha."

As they greeted one another Dina was thinking, "What a fine-looking young man is this Yitzhak. Who knows? Maybe someday we will make a *shidoch* (arranged marriage) with him and one of our daughters. How good it would be to have a farmer for a relative!"

Dina began the bargaining and bartering with Shlomo Charkoff for his fine vegetables. She paid a small amount of money, but wanting to get more for her family, she also offered to help Mrs. Charkoff with some sewing she needed. Then, when she noticed how old their mezuzah was, she asked Shlomo, "Do you think you might need a new parchment for your *mezuzah*?[9]"

Laughing as he said it, Charkoff responded, "Dina, you have a good head for business. Yes, actually I was thinking about getting a new mezuzah parchment. I'll tell you what. For your help with the curtains and the mezuzah I'll bring you a nice goose for your next Shabbos dinner."

Dina was pleased and thanked Shlomo. As Shayna Chaya and Sura Basha loaded their baskets with the fine turnips, beets, potatoes, and cabbages, Moshe sprang into action, helping the girls gather and load the produce. He couldn't resist the urge to show off, and grabbed some potatoes and began juggling them. When all three fell to the ground, the girls giggled and Charkoff frowned at his son's antics. Dina and her daughters walked home in the cool of the evening, after enjoying the cabbage borscht Mrs. Charkoff had offered them.

The mother of seven children, Dina had grown to be considered a *balabusta* (literally, a good homemaker) and an enterprising businesswoman. She routinely walked to the surrounding villages and farms to buy food and other items she knew were in demand, and then sold them from her home in Losice.

Hers was a life of constant toil. In addition to raising her children in a strictly orthodox home with the demands of a kosher kitchen, the elaborate

---

[9] A Mezuzah is a small narrow container attached to the doorpost of Jewish homes. The little piece of parchment inside includes two prayers taken from Deuteronomy 6:4-9 and 11:13-21. The second is especially important to farmers, because the text includes the words of God, "And I will place rain for your land in its proper time, the early and the late rains, that you may gather in your grain, your wine, and your oil. And I will provide grass in your field for your cattle, and you will eat and you will be satisfied."

preparations necessary each and every Friday to prepare for Shabbos, and having to go to the *mikvah* (ritual bath house) at the times of the month prescribed in connection with her menstrual cycle, she also had to keep the house quiet so her husband, Chaim, could concentrate on his very exacting work as a sofer.

Chapter 48

An Unwelcome Visitor

Perl and Minicha rushed out of their apartment to welcome their mother and sisters and help them carry their load into the kitchen. Shayna and Sura Basha excitedly told them all about their visit to the farm, as they helped Dina separate the food they would keep for the house and the items they expected to sell. Then, with the help of her daughters, Dina prepared the evening meal of soup with knedlach, boiled chicken, stewed cabbage, kasha, and a freshly baked challah. Stewed prunes and mandel broit were to be the dessert.

As the daughters and their brother Natan ate their dinner, Dina noticed that Chaim, who was ordinarily a tranquil person, seemed nervous and on edge. He ate little and spoke hardly at all during the meal, other than offering the blessings before and after the meal. But, at one point, uncharacteristically, he spoke harshly to his daughters, shouting at them to be quiet. They had still been chattering about their trip to the farm.

After dinner the daughters cleared the table and Natan left the apartment to visit a friend in the neighborhood. Dina was concerned, wondering what could possibly have happened to her usually serene husband. She bent down and whispered in his ear, "Chaim, shall we go into the other room to talk?"

"Yes, let us do that," he said. "I have something very important to discuss with you, but first I will tell you what happened here today and you'll understand why I am so upset. At about twelve o'clock I heard a loud noise coming from across the street. I went out to see what was happening. Our *meshugana* (crazy) Polish neighbor, Symanowski, who is always trying to make trouble for us, was shouting that someone had stolen three of his chickens. Of course, everyone on the street knows that his chickens often get loose and wander all over the neighborhood. I came out of the house to find out what was wrong. By that time a crowd had gathered. As soon as he saw me he pointed his finger at me and started to scream, 'He did it. He stole my beautiful chickens!'"

Dina was outraged and said, "Oh, dear God. So tell me, what did you do?"

"Do?" Chaim protested. "I did nothing. What can you do when you are dealing with a crazy man?"

"So what happened next?" Dina asked.

"Well, I had a little *mazel* (good luck) for a change. Just then that nice Constable Kaczmarski came walking down our street. When he found out what Symanowski was shouting about, the Constable told him to calm down and that he would investigate the matter. He came over to me and suggested that we go into our apartment. He could see I was upset, so when we were alone he told me he knew all about our crazy neighbor. He also told me he knew that I was an honorable and highly respected man in the Jewish community and not to worry. He would take care of Symanowski his own way. I offered him a schnapps. He drank it straight down and then had another. I put out some of your mandel broit. He stuffed his pockets with them and left."

"Thank God Constable Kaczmarski came along just then. I don't care if he's not Jewish, he is such a *mensch* (fine person). Otherwise there could have been trouble." Dina shook her head.

Chaim nodded in agreement. He sat there quietly for a minute or two, deep in thought. Then he said the words Dina had been waiting to hear.

"Dina, we must go to America." He went on to explain, "Today's latest problem reminded me that even though our families have been living here in this shtetl for many generations, during that time there has always been the worry of one kind of trouble or another from people who hate us for no other reason than that we are Jews. If there is a better place to live in this world, where we can feel safe, then we must go there. I will write to our sons tonight. They said they would send us the money to make the trip."

"Thank you, Chaim. Your words are words of wisdom. I will tell the children."

Natan was still away, so Dina asked the girls to sit down at the dining table. She said, "I have some important news to tell you. Your wise and wonderful father has decided that we will go to America."

Shayna Chaya and Sura Basha hugged one another and then hugged their mother. Perl and Minicha, the two younger daughters, seemed dazed by the news, because they didn't fully comprehend what it would all mean. But seeing the joy expressed by their mother and sisters, they soon joined in the celebration, as Dina pulled them to her and kissed all of them.

After a while, when the celebration had calmed down, Dina said, "There will be a great deal to do and we will all have to work very hard to get ready."

Just then they were all startled by a loud knock on the door. It sounded like someone was banging on it with a heavy stick.

Chaim went to the door and opened it. A tall, blond, mustachioed Polish army officer stood there a moment, and then stepped briskly inside. In his left hand he clutched an elaborately carved cane with an ivory handle. He wore a leather holster with a shiny silver pistol on his right side.

"I am Lieutenant Korzinski," he declared in a booming voice. "You are the Jew Zynger, are you not?" he snarled.

Dina quietly told her daughters to go into the other room as Chaim responded, "Yes, this is the Zynger family. How can I help you, Officer Korzinski?'"

"According to the records of this village you have four sons and none of them have served in the glorious Polish army. Of course, we understand the needs of a family, even a Jew family, so we have exempted your oldest son, Elijah." Korzinski was trying to sound sincere, but not succeeding.

Chaim then said, "We would appreciate that gesture if it were not true that our dear sweet Elijah, of blessed memory, died long ago when he was just a boy of ten."

Moving on without regard for what he had just heard, the Lieutenant asked, "And what of your son Israel?"

"In America," answered Chaim.

"And let me see," the officer said, as Korzinski looked over his notes. "So what about Herschel?"

"Also in America."

At this point both Chaim and Dina were holding on to the hope that the lieutenant did not have Natan's name on his list. They knew too well what would happen to Natan if he were to be called. He would be conscripted into an army where, because he was a Jew, he would be bullied and abused by men like the pompous, arrogant Lieutenant Korzinski who stood before them.

Then, after taking a torturously long look through his notes, Korzinsky asked smugly, "And what of your son Natan, has he also left to become a Yankee?"

Dina and Chaim felt their hearts sink as Chaim, knowing there was no choice, declared, "He is not at home right now."

Korzinski took out a piece of paper, wrote a few words on it, and handed it to Chaim, saying, "Have him report to this address no later than seven tomorrow morning."

With that he quickly turned and strode out the door, leaving the scene of devastation without a further thought.

Chapter 49

Gloom and Then Hope

Ever since that terrible morning when Natan left for his doomed fate as a member of the Polish army, the Zynger household had been in a state of shock and depression. Natan put on his bravest face that morning as everyone in the family bid him a tearful farewell. But in truth he was terrified. All his life he had heard horror stories of how cruel the army was to young Jewish men. And now he was to be one of those unfortunates.

Even though there was the trip to America to look forward to and a thousand chores to be completed, keeping them occupied day and night, there was a pervasive gloom in the house. Having to sort out what they would take, what was to be sold, what was to be given to relatives and friends, and what was to go to the poor helped to distract them just a little. Everyone walked about with sober faces, as if "the evil eye" was upon them. Seven-year-old Menicha often cried herself to sleep. She sorely missed the only one of her three brothers she knew.

On the day when the money for the trip reached them, though that should have been a reason for celebration, they knew it only brought them closer to the moment when they would be leaving Natan alone in Poland while they traveled thousands of miles away. Israel and Herschel had sent the princely sum of twelve hundred dollars for the journey, an amount that would be the equivalent of more than twenty thousand dollars today. It was more money than any of them expected to see in a lifetime!

Though no formal announcement was made, not even at their synagogue, the news that they would be leaving Losice for America spread very quickly throughout the Jewish community. Their rabbi was devastated when he realized that the greatest Torah scholar and teacher in the congregation would be lost to them forever. Chaim gathered together his prayer books and Torah-writing materials with a heavy heart, picking up this and then that and weeping quietly and privately so as not to be seen by his daughters.

It is not known exactly what was done with the apartment house they owned. It may be that Avrum Binstock bought it from them, or that it was given to another relative with some kind of financial arrangement. However, owning the apartment would not turn out to be a blessing, because it would have obligated the owner to remain as caretaker to the property, instead of considering moving away. At the time the Zynger family left Poland they could not have imagined the horror that would befall their relatives and neighbors. Almost no Jew alive in Losice at that time, who remained in Poland, would live more than twenty-one more years.

As the time to leave grew closer, there was a change in Dina's demeanor. Each day she grew less and less gloomy and more and more cheerful. Chaim couldn't understand her behavior. Finally, late one night in bed she turned to him and said, "Don't worry, my husband, I think I have found a way to use the money that was sent to us to rescue Natan."

Chaim was surprised but hopeful as he replied, "Dina, how could we do such a thing? It doesn't seem possible."

"Chaim, I have a plan. No matter what else happens I intend to carry it out. I cannot bear the idea of leaving Natan to his fate. As with all of our children, he is precious to us, so deeply embedded in our hearts. First, we lost our young Yitzchak to sickness and then we had to send two of our wonderful sons away because of the accursed army conscription. We cannot lose Natan as well. Here is what I intend to do."

She proceeded to outline her plan. As she laid it out for him, Chaim was astonished by what his amazing wife was planning, and even more, by the amount of chutzpah he knew would be needed to carry out her scheme. At first he argued that the plan was too dangerous and might put the whole family in peril. But Dina was steadfast in her determination. Perhaps it also seems odd that Chaim did not insist on carrying out the plan himself, after all he was the "man of the house." But instead, he went along with an action that could potentially put his wife and all of them in danger. Not only did he understand how determined Dina could be once her mind was made up, but he also understood that with her plan a woman would have a better chance of succeeding than a man.

The next day she asked her big burly-bearded cousin Mordechai to accompany her to the home of Nachman Lewinski, a printer well known to her family, whose shop was many blocks away from their home. It was in a bleak, dreary section of Losice, where there were a few small businesses and some aging run-down warehouses. It was perilous for a woman to enter this area unaccompanied by a man. This visit was to be the first step in her bold and daring plan to rescue Natan.

Chapter 50

Step One: The Visa

Dina and Mordechai entered the small, cluttered print shop of Nachman Lewinski, the aged printer. He was a grey-bearded old man, stooped over from years spent proofing his work up close, to be certain of its perfection. He wore a black yarmulke on his balding head.

He peered at them through the thick lenses of his glasses, with a look of surprise. Dina was always amused by the way Nachman Lewinski, who possessed a high, nasally voice, had the habit of speaking effusively, frequently repeating himself, his words bubbling out like foam pouring over the lip of a glass of beer.

"Dina," he declared. "I am very surprised, oh my, so surprised and honored, yes, yes, I'm honored to have you visit my place of business. And how is my old friend Chaim? Oh, I have so much admiration for your husband. Yes, yes, he is such a great sofer. His Torahs are masterpieces, masterpieces I tell you. I have never ever ever seen such perfection. Please give my regards to Chaim, oh yes, you must give him my regards. And this is your cousin, a member of the Oxengoren family, is he not? Yes, yes, he's your cousin, isn't he?"

"Yes, Nachman, this is my cousin Mordechai. I asked him to accompany me. And tell me, how is Mrs. Lewinski?" Dina asked with a look of concern.

"Much better, thank you. Oh yes, yes she is much, much better," he answered. "I have hot water in my samovar. Can I get both of you some tea? How about a nice cup of hot tea, what do you say?"

"No, thank you very much. We haven't much time and I have a great favor to ask of you." She spoke the words with a sense of urgency.

"Of course," he said, looking disappointed that his offer of tea was not accepted. "Please ask. Go ahead and ask. If I can help you, I will. Yes, I most certainly will. Yes, please ask."

Dina then explained the situation: about how the family was planning to go to America and that their son Natan was suddenly taken by the Polish army. The printer, who was an old and dear friend of the Zynger family, nodded his head in sympathy when Dina told him she was determined to get Natan out of the army and send him to America.

Before she finished, he interrupted, saying, "You want my help to print a visa for him, don't you? Yes, yes, I guessed that right away, right away."

"Yes," she replied. "Nachman, can you do that for us? I heard that you have been known to do such a thing and that you do a wonderful job. We can pay you well."

Lewinski answered by asking another question. "Do you have your own visa with you? If you do, can you show it to me? Let's have a look at it. Pay, you say? Nonsense, no pay, no pay, nonsense. It's a privilege to help you…yes, yes, a great privilege."

Dina, relief written on her face, reached into the bag she was carrying and pulled out her visa. Lewinski picked up his magnifying glass and studied it for several minutes. As he looked up with a smile he said, "Yes, yes, I can make an exact duplicate for your son. It will be exact and perfect. They'll never know the difference. You know, that's how it has to be, so that's how it's going to be. You see, I have this old friend. I've known him for a thousand years. He worked for the government. Yes, he worked for the government and gave me some of the special paper they use for visas, so I'm ready to go. Yes, yes, I'm ready to go, and as it happens right now business is slow, so I will get to work on this today. Dina, I know you'll be busy getting ready for Shabbos, won't you? Yes, yes, you'll be busy with Shabbos, but perhaps Mordechai can come. Mordechai, you can come, yes?"

Mordechai nodded.

"You should be here at noon on Friday. Yes, yes, it will be ready by noon on Friday and I'll give you some tea and some of my wife's apple strudel…tea and apple strudel and…the new visa!"

Mordechai, a fine young man but not much of a talker, nodded in agreement and then Dina said to the printer, "God bless you! Such a mitzvah!"

Chapter 51

The Basket

At Dina's request, Chaim called on a merchant he knew who provided supplies to the army post on the outskirts of Losice, where Natan was serving. He was to make an inquiry. Dina wanted to learn who Natan's commanding officer was, and anything they could find out about him. Chaim found out that Lieutenant Korzinsky, the strutting peacock who came to their house to snatch Natan up, was his commanding officer. However, he wasn't on duty every day. A younger Lieutenant Kovach was the acting commander on Mondays and Tuesdays. He also learned that Kovach was a married man with a family, while Korzinsky was a bachelor.

On Sunday, the day before they were to leave, Dina prepared a basket. It was filled with pastries including poppyseed hamentaschen, sugar cookies, apple strudel, honey cake, a freshly baked challah, a bottle of schnapps, and, tucked down at the very bottom, an envelope stuffed with rubles. Again, she enlisted the help of her burly but quiet cousin Mordechai. He carried the basket for her and acted as a sort of bodyguard. Chaim remained at home to supervise their daughters in preparing for the great move the next day. Dina hired a carriage to take her and Mordechai to the army post, located twenty kilometers north of Losice. Motorized vehicles were not yet common in Losice.

When they reached the gate, a sentry asked them to state their business. Dina was nervous and a bit frightened but determined to go through with her plan no matter what. She answered the sentry, "We are here to see Lieutenant Kovach on an urgent matter."

"State your name," the sentry demanded.

"I am Mrs. Dina Zynger," she responded, feeling a special pride in saying those words.

The sentry picked up his rifle and quickly turned and marched to the building behind him.

It was a hot fall day, the sun was beating down and bees were buzzing about. They waited and waited. Fifteen, twenty minutes passed. Finally, the sentry returned and said, "Follow me."

Dina almost lost her courage as she entered the gloomy building. But when she looked over at Mordechai, he smiled and gave her an encouraging nod. It gave her a boost of courage and a sense of calm came over her. The sentry knocked on the commander's door. "Enter," they heard.

Dina and Mordechai walked into the sparsely furnished office. Two tired old chairs stood against one of the walls, painted a nondescript shade of brown. The commander's oak desk and chair were before them and a Polish flag was near one of the two small windows. There were some official-looking papers on the desk and a framed family photo. Lieutenant Kovach—a short, stocky man in his late thirties, with closely trimmed light blond hair—stood as they entered.

"I am Lieutenant Kovach. You say you have urgent business? Perhaps it is urgent for you but not for the army."

"Lieutenant Kovach, I am Mrs. Dina Zynger and this is my cousin Mordechai Oxengoren."

Mordechai nodded to Kovach. When Lieutenant Kovach noticed the basket Mordechai was carrying, his manner softened and he said, "Tell me about this urgent matter. Perhaps I can help."

"Well, you see, sir, my son Natan is one of your soldiers. Our family is moving to America. We will be going to Warsaw tomorrow for three days to arrange to take the train. After we leave we won't be able to see him for a very long time, if ever again. Please, sir, can you let him come with us to Warsaw to see us off and say a proper good-bye? Perhaps a leave of four or five days? I see by the picture on your desk that you have a family. If you have a son of your own, I am sure you must know how we feel."

Kovach sat back down. He tapped the desk with the fingers of his right hand and appeared to be deep in thought. Then he looked over at the basket and, ignoring Dina's request for the moment, he asked, "What do you have in that fine-looking basket?"

Dina motioned for Mordechai to take it to the desk. Then she said, "These are just a few little things, to express our thanks for your service to our country. There are some sweet cakes and cookies, a freshly baked bread, and a bottle of Slivovitz, to keep a soldier's stomach warm on cold winter nights."

The lieutenant, his curiosity piqued, stood up and peered into the basket, picking up various items and examining them. Then he noticed the envelope at the bottom. He withdrew it and quickly estimated the amount of money in it, then reluctantly replaced it in the basket.

Smiling broadly, Kovach said, "And the money?"

"Oh," Dina said. "That is so the soldier could buy a nice gift for his mother or his wife." Dina felt her confidence building and her hope for success growing.

"You say four days, and then he will return? How can I be sure he will return?"

Throwing her arms out, palms up, she said as emphatically as she could, "What could we do? After all, he is in the army."

Kovach nodded and said, "Yes, that is true. Just remember that."

The lieutenant walked to the door of his office. He summoned his assistant, giving him instructions. Then he turned to Dina and Mordechai, saying, "I'm going to see what we can do."

Lieutenant Kovach invited Dina and Mordechai to sit in his office and wait. Ten minutes passed. The assistant returned. Kovach and the soldier had a confidential conversation just outside the office door, which Dina could not hear. The lieutenant returned to the office, frowning, and said, "Sometimes in this army we can't have control over everything. You just never know what is going to happen from day to day."

Dina and Mordechai looked at each other, alarmed at the lieutenant's words. The tension built as Kovach continued, "Early this morning there was a terrible accident on the base. Two of our soldiers were killed. They had mishandled some explosives. Two Jews, your son and another Jew"—as he spoke these words, Dina caught her breath, pounded her chest, and turned pale— "have been assigned the job of digging the graves. I'm afraid that your son will not be able to leave until he and the other Jew complete the job."

"But you said you would see what you could do! Can't you get another soldier to dig the graves? You have a lot of soldiers. Surely someone else could do it," Dina pleaded.

"I'm sorry, but I cannot countermand that order."

As he said that, Dina moved over to the basket. She reached out and clutched the handle. The lieutenant put his hand on another part of the basket handle, gently pulling it toward him. Summoning his most sincere tone of voice, he looked earnestly at Dina, explaining, "I will see to it that your son is permitted to leave the instant he has completed the work. You have my word on that as an officer of the glorious Polish army!"

Dina held on to the basket and said, "Very well, but before we leave I want to talk to my son, so he knows about our trip tomorrow. Can you please get someone to bring him here? I just need a minute or two to speak to him."

Looking annoyed, the Lieutenant answered, "All right, all right, I'll send someone for him, but he must start the digging right away, so please do keep it to a minute or two. Wait for him by the main gate, where you came in."

As Dina removed her hand from the basket, with the hint of a smile on her face she said, "I hope the soldier who receives this basket enjoys it very much and remembers who gave it to him and why."

The lieutenant opened the door. Dina and Mordechai walked back to the main gate.

In a few minutes, Natan appeared. His mother hugged and kissed him, and as she did so she whispered in his ear, "Natan, you must finish digging the graves by tomorrow morning. Someone will come to get you about ten o'clock. We are leaving for Warsaw tomorrow morning. When we get there we will put you on a train to Belgium so you can leave this country forever. It has all been arranged. Do you understand?"

Natan, astonished, nodded and asked, "But how...?"

Before he could finish, Dina hushed him, saying, "All will be explained when you join us. Somehow, my son, you must find the strength to finish your terrible job by tomorrow morning."

With that, she kissed him again. Dina tearfully turned and she and Mordechai left, not knowing with any certainty whether they had actually succeeded in their mission.

Chapter 52

Hard Labor

Natan purposely avoided telling his mother who the other Jewish grave-digger was to be. His name was Mendel. Natan knew Mendel would not be good at digging graves or anything that required physical labor. He was also aware that his mother knew the same thing about Mendel. He didn't want to additionally distress her.

Mendel was a *Yeshiva Bocher* (an orthodox religious school student). That meant he spent almost all of his time studying the *Torah*, the *Talmud*, and the *Mishna*. He was a tall, pencil-thin, pale, and frail boy of seventeen. He had a long neck, a protruding Adam's apple, a bony hooked nose, and curly black hair to complete the forlorn picture.

Mendel happened to be in the wrong place at the worst time, when the army was in need of filling their conscript quota. Mendel's knowledge of the holy books at such a young age was legendary in the Jewish community, but would not be of help in this situation.

Natan, while not a model physical specimen, had a stocky build. Being the only son in the Zynger house for the past few years since Herschel left for America, he usually did the heaviest physical work needed in the house: carrying the wood for the stove, and all the heavy items that needed moving from here to there.

Soldier Wojkowski's selection of the two young Jews to do the physically demanding job of digging two graves was cruelly cynical. They had only been in the army a short time and had had very little opportunity to be toughened up. But that wasn't the only factor in this case. Since the army didn't concern itself with the religious practices of Jews, they didn't provide the kosher food that those recruits could or would eat. This left them weak and undernourished, since they could only eat eggs, fruits, and vegetables. Wojkowski was the most anti-Semitic man at the army post and wanted to use this grave-digging opportunity to express his hatred, by breaking the spirit of these two unfortunate young men.

The two explosion victims were to be buried on the grounds of the army post in a small cemetery in the far corner of the property. One of them was an orphan with no known family. The other had a family that so far could not be located.

Natan and Mendel were taken to a shed, where Wojkowski told them to get a wheelbarrow, shovels, pickaxes, wooden stakes, a measuring stick, some twine, and a ladder. He gave them five minutes of instruction and sent them on their way, fiendishly laughing as he watched them trudge off into the distance.

It was another warm day that would get hotter with the afternoon sun. Natan, with Mendel's help, measured the area for the first grave. He drove the stakes in and tied the twine around the perimeter of the area to be dug. Then they both started to dig. The top soil was fairly soft. Natan's shovel sliced into the earth with some ease, but Mendel, with his weak, bony arms, could barely scrape an inch of dirt away, and try as he might, he made no real progress. When Natan was down two feet, Mendel was still scraping away at the first inch or two.

Finally, Natan, resting on his shovel, turned to Mendel and said, "I think you should be doing a different job. You are not suited to do this work, are you?"

Mendel, in tears, sobbed, "But what else is there that I could do?"

"You can be my helper," Natan declared.

"But how can I help you, Natan?"

"Well, let's see. When I have loosened the earth, you can pick up as much as you can handle and put it into the pile next to the grave. You can get me water when I need it and you can go over to the post and bring us our food. That would be a great help. And you could tell me about your studies of the Talmud and the teachings of the great rabbis, to help pass the time."

And so, each of them did what they were most capable of doing. Natan made good progress until he cleared all of the top soil. Then he came to a thick layer of dense gray clay, which had to be broken apart piece by piece with the pickaxe. The sun blazed and there was no breeze to cool him.

Mendel walked the quarter of a mile each way for a pail of water. Natan gulped the water directly from the pail and splashed some on his head. Then he went back to work.

The skin on his hands was not hardened like that of a laborer and he was unaccustomed to handling shovels and picks. Blisters broke out on his hands, but he resolved to ignore them. He was driven by the elemental instinct of self-survival, for he had become convinced that Wojkowski would not let up until he was dead. He knew he must complete the job. If he couldn't leave the camp tomorrow he would surely die in this place.

He continued to dig without a break for three more hours, while Mendel regaled him with his vast knowledge of Rabbis Akiva, Eleazar, Rashi, Ramban, and the Vilna Gaon. Of course, Natan's own father, Chaim, had filled him with Jewish knowledge, but there was always something new that could be learned.

At about six, Mendel trudged back to the post and returned with dinner: a bowl of cold potato soup, some black bread, and an apple. After downing the food Natan got back to work again. By that time his back was aching and his hands were bleeding.

As the sun set and it grew dark, Natan felt a sense of panic. Night was rapidly approaching and he wasn't as yet finished with the first grave. He was thoroughly exhausted and gripping the shovel was becoming more painful each minute. He was about one foot short of being finished with the first grave when it grew so dark he could no longer continue. Mendel lowered the small ladder and Natan climbed out of the grave. He had begun to believe the grave was meant for him.

As they stumbled over the field in the dark, Natan told Mendel about the four-day leave he was hoping to get, but didn't reveal his plan to go absent without leave. He didn't want Mendel to have any knowledge about his plan that he might reveal accidentally or under duress. He also knew that Mendel would be very upset to learn that Natan would not be returning. During the course of the day's adversity the two boys had grown close. Natan's heart ached when thinking about what lay ahead for this delicate young boy, a person he cared about, a fellow Jew, a friend. As they moved closer to the barracks, Natan asked, "Mendel, do you believe in miracles?"

"Of course, Natan, the Torah is full of God's wonderful miracles: the parting of the Red Sea, the burning bush, water from the rock, the giving of the Ten Commandments, Daniel in the lion's den, and so many more."

"Yes," said Natan, "but those all happened a very long time ago. Do you think God still makes miracles?"

"Yes, I do," responded Mendel with confidence, "especially if the need is great and important."

"Well, Mendel, I don't know if the need is great enough or important enough, but I think the only way we will be able to finish the graves by ten o'clock tomorrow is with the help of one of God's miracles. Do you think it would be alright if we both prayed for a miracle?"

"Why not, Natan? One of the great rabbis declared that while it is not appropriate to pray in all situations, it cannot hurt to do so. I will pray for that miracle and for deliverance from this burden for both of us."

They dragged themselves into the barracks, collapsed into their rough bunks, and prayed to God for that miracle.

Chapter 53

A Surprising Development

Natan sank into his bunk in a state of total exhaustion. He closed his eyes. His mind wandered into that space somewhere between a thought, a wish, and perhaps a dream, where he wasn't certain which of them he was floating through. Mendel was there before him, transformed into a larger man with great spirit, strength, and a body of bulging muscles. Mendel was digging the second grave furiously. Natan and he had changed roles. He was the one piling the loose soil next to the grave and then carrying a pail of water and giving it to Mendel. There was a hint of a smile on Natan's face as he slipped into the deep sleep of exhaustion.

The next sound heard was the dawn crowing of a rooster somewhere in the distance. For a moment Natan couldn't recall where he was. Then he remembered and groaned as he pulled himself off the bunk, every muscle and joint in his body protesting his slightest movement. He willed himself to stand and, reaching over with his aching arm, shook Mendel's shoulder. They slowly and silently dressed and slipped out into the cool morning air. The nearly full moon was still hanging low in the sky and dawn's first light was hinting at the sun's approaching emergence.

When they reached the grave, they both stood for a moment, looking at what was ahead of them that day, and slowly climbed down into the cold, damp earth. Somehow Natan was able to work his sore muscles and loosen the soil. Within an hour they had finally finished the first grave. With grim determination they pulled the stakes out of the ground and began the process of laying out their second task. With Natan's physical condition it felt beyond hope.

They had just begun to measure out the space when two soldiers approached. The one they knew, named Gorski, shouted to them, "Stop what you are doing. You have been ordered to go to the office of Lieutenant Kovach immediately."

Natan and Pinchas looked at one another and just stood still for a moment, wondering what other terrible thing was about to happen. Gorski shouted at them, "Why are you waiting? Go, go now!"

Natan and Mendel trudged to the office of Lieutenant Kovach with trepidation. After they had gone a short distance, Natan turned around to see if Gorski and the other soldier were behind them. He was surprised to discover that instead of following, the soldiers were gathering up the tools and loading them on to the wheelbarrow. He wondered, "What is happening and why?"

When they reached the headquarters building, Lieutenant Kovach's assistant told them to stand by the wall and wait. Loud voices seeped through the thin walls of Kovach's office. One of them sounded like their nemesis, Wojkowski. What was obviously an argument went on for a minute or two. Then there was a loud bang like the sound of a fist hitting a desk or a table and the words "Get out" could be heard. The door to the office flung open. Wojkowski charged out. He saw the two men and snarled like a rabid dog as he left the building.

The men were told to go into Kovach's office. They were thoroughly confused, their heads swimming with unanswered questions. They saluted Kovach, who stood up and asked them, "How far along are you in your assignment?"

"We have finished one of the graves, sir," Natan answered.

"Very well then, your task is finished." Looking at Mendel, he said, "You may go to your barracks."

Mendel did not move, but waited to see what would be said to Natan. Kovach reached into his desk and pulled out a piece of paper, on which he wrote a note. As he handed it to Natan he said, "This is your four-day pass. See to it that you return by this time on Friday."

As Natan reached out to accept the pass he wondered if he dared ask why they did not have to dig the second grave. He thanked Kovach for the pass and somehow controlled his curiosity. The two men turned to leave and had reached the door when Kovach quietly stated, "A brother of one of the soldiers who was killed came here early this morning to claim his body."

Natan and Mendel looked at one another and slowly nodded their heads as they left the building. Mendel bid good-bye to Natan, saying, "Please tell your esteemed father and your family that I hope God will bless them with a safe journey to America. I'm looking forward to hearing about your trip to Warsaw when you return on Friday."

Natan couldn't bear to look at Mendel, but as he turned toward the main gate he responded quietly, "Yes, I'll give my family your message." At the same time he made a pledge to himself. Before he left Poland he would find a way to get in touch with Mendel's family and urge them to do whatever they could to get him out of the army.

As he reached the front gate, a group of soldiers talking loudly passed by. At the same time, he wasn't sure, but thought he heard someone call his name. Natan handed his pass to the sentry, who read it and handed it back. Then, just as he was set to walk through the gate to freedom at last, the sentry stepped in front of him and commanded, "Stop, you are being summoned."

He turned to see Kovach's assistant briskly striding toward him. Once again, Natan was filled with foreboding.

"Soldier Zynger, announced the approaching soldier, "I have a message for you from Lieutenant Kovach. You are to tell your mother that the soldier and his family who received the basket enjoyed it very much and they thank her for her kindness."

Natan had no idea what the man was talking about, but quickly responded, "Thank you, I'll give her the message."

Once again Natan turned toward the gate. This time the sentry stepped aside. Natan walked toward the road. He hadn't thought for even a moment of first returning to gather any of his clothing or personal belongings before he left. His only thought was to pass through that gate. But by that time all that had happened to him over the past twenty-four hours began to take its toll. He and Mendel had left early that morning before they had a chance to eat or drink anything. Natan was malnourished and dehydrated, and although he felt euphoric to know he was now, at last, on his way to join his beloved family, his overburdened body rebelled.

As he approached the road, Natan became confused and couldn't remember whether to turn right or left. He remembered that his mother told him someone would come for him at ten o'clock, but he resolved to walk down the road and meet them on their way. He was determined to not spend one more moment at the army post. In his confused state, he mistakenly turned to the right and set off down the road going the wrong way, growing weaker with every step.

As he walked along, Natan's eye was drawn to a beautiful yellow shadow butterfly flitting about above him, as if leading him forward to freedom. Several minutes passed. Now disoriented and dizzy, he stumbled and fell. The dizziness increased. The butterfly flapped its wings. He thought to himself, "I'll sit here and rest a while." Seated on a grassy area next to the road, Natan gazed up at the yellow wings. That was the last thing he remembered until....

Chapter 54

The Procession

The day had finally arrived. The Zynger family would be leaving the homeland they had known for generations. They would be traveling thousands of miles, over land and sea, to a strange land where they would have to learn a new language and live a different life than they had ever known.

Chaim had arranged to have a member of their synagogue, Perchik Levy, transport them all the way to Warsaw, in his large wagon drawn by two sturdy horses. When they reached Warsaw, Levy would buy merchandise he could sell when he returned to Losice in a few days. The family had loaded all of their bags and baskets, along with a large steamer trunk they had purchased for the trip. In addition to Chaim and Dina and hopefully Natan, and their four daughters, traveling with them were a niece, Malka, and a nephew, Jacob, the children of Chaim's sister Hynda, who remained behind for several more years.

The busy scene in front of their apartment might have been mistaken for a celebration, because of the number of people who had gathered there on that morning. But instead, it was a sad day for the Jews of Losice. Their highly respected sofer and Torah scholar was leaving, along with his family, one that held a prominent place in the Jewish community. It was an expression of deep respect that so many friends, relatives, and neighbors came to say good-bye and wish them well.

At eight o'clock that morning Mordechai pulled up in a carriage and Chaim climbed into it. They were setting off to pick up Natan from the army camp as planned, desperately hoping he would be waiting for them at the gate. They planned to meet the wagon with the rest of the family at a designated place west of Losice on the Warsaw road.

At about ten o'clock that morning, Perchik Levy urged his horses to move and the procession began. And a procession is what it was. Stretched out along the narrow streets, as many as seventy men, women, and children solemnly followed the slow-moving wagon through and out of the town.

In the closing scene of the magnificent musical *Fiddler on the Roof*, based on Yiddish author Sholem Aleichem's book "Tevye's Daughters," Tevye's family is leaving their beloved home in Anatevka, with most of the Jews of the shtetl following their wagon out of town as they sing their sad refrain.

According to the members of the Singer family, the scene as they left Losice that morning could have been scripted the same way as Sholem Aleichem's tale.

In the meantime, Chaim and Mordechai had reached the army post. They pulled up to the gate and climbed down from the carriage. The sentry saw them approaching and asked them to state their business.

"We are here to meet the soldier Natan Zynger. Do you know if he is ready to leave?"

The sentry looked the two of them over disdainfully and mumbled, "Did you say the Jew Zynger? I think he left more than an hour ago."

Chaim, very concerned when he heard the answer, said, "But we didn't see him on the road. Are you sure it was Zynger and that he left already?"

The irritable sentry answered, "Yes, I'm sure, now if you have no further questions go away!"

Chaim turned around and had a discussion with Mordechai. After a moment they both nodded in agreement, and Chaim turned to the sentry again, asking, "Do you remember which way he went, to the right or the left?"

Sensing an economic opportunity, the sentry replied, "I'm having trouble recalling which way went, perhaps you can think of something that might help improve my memory?"

Chaim was puzzled by the sentry's answer, but Mordechai said two words to him. Chaim nodded that he understood, reached into his pocket, pulled out a few coins, and pressed them into the hand of the sentry, who happily declared, "Yes, I remember now. He went to the right." Chaim and Mordechai quickly climbed back into the carriage and headed down the road to the right.

Later Natan was recalling what he remembered of that day. In his semi-conscious state he heard voices and felt someone picking him up. Then he was bumping along in a wagon or carriage of some kind. Someone opened his mouth and spilled schnapps down his throat. It burned and shocked him as it went down.

As he opened his eyes, all he discerned at first was a misty fog. Gradually his eyes focused and he realized he was looking at a cloud-covered sky. His head was resting on something soft and warm. He looked around and saw his sister Sura Basha looking down at him with a warm smile. His head was on her lap. Shayna was soothingly applying a damp cloth to his forehead, while Perl and Menicha were joyfully shouting, "Natan's awake, Natan's awake!" The sisters vied with one another, competing to do what they could for Natan, bringing him water, food, and comfort.

By that time they were a few kilometers east of Losice. All those who had been in the procession had said their good-byes and sadly turned back home. It was Chaim who had dug through the big trunk and found the bottle of schnapps he used to revive Natan. Mordechai had returned to Losice.

Shortly after Natan had become fully conscious, he became very agitated. He called for his mother and father and began to plead with them to return to Losice so he could talk to Mendel's family. When he told them the reason, they were very sympathetic but said they could not turn back now. However, they asked Natan to tell his story about Mendel to Perchik Levy, their wagon driver. Perchik listened with great interest, nodding several times to indicate that he understood the urgency of the message. He vowed to deliver Natan's message as soon as he returned from Warsaw. Natan, though still worried, thanked Perchik and was somewhat relieved. He would remind Perchik about the message several more times on the trip.

They moved along on the road to Warsaw slowly but steadily until late in the afternoon, as the sky darkened and the wind bent the trees and grasses. Chaim and Perchik considered places where they could stop for the night and hopefully find shelter before the impending storm struck.

Minicha was sitting on a box in the rear of the big wagon playing with a doll, and every once in a while looking back at the road behind them. As she peered at the horizon she saw something moving briskly in their direction. Her eyes grew wider as she stared at the bouncing image. Waiting until it drew closer so she could be sure of what it was, she became frightened and screamed, "Soldiers! Soldiers on horses are coming!"

Chapter 55

The Storm

At Minicha's loud cry, everyone on the wagon turned around to see why she was screaming. Minicha was right to be alarmed. Far off to the east, and riding furiously in their direction, they could make out a group of three or four Polish cavalrymen, coming down the road at a full gallop. Dina, terror-struck, turned to Chaim and then to Perchik, the wagon driver, and asked them, "What shall we do?"

Chaim answered first, "There is nothing we can do. I'm certain they have seen us. We know we have done nothing wrong. Natan has his pass from the army. We must remain calm. Dina, please tell the children everything will be alright and that if the soldiers stop and ask any questions they should just be quiet."

Then Perchik, who had traversed that road to Warsaw many times, said, "I don't think you have to worry, those young fools may just be racing their horses to prove who is the best rider."

Natan put his hand on the four-day pass, to be certain he had it ready to show, if needed. At the same time, Dina felt the lining of her coat, where she had sewn Natan's forged visa.

But another matter was beginning to greatly concern everyone on the open, uncovered wagon. The cloudy sky had turned ominously dark. The wind had died down to a "calm before the storm" state. A flash of lightning sparked far to the north. The sky was rapidly changing color, to the foreboding pale-yellowish hue that precedes major storms. The first roar of thunder shook the earth, like the vibrations of a train rushing by at full throttle. At the same time, the drumming beat of galloping horses was growing stronger and the four riders could be seen clearly as they churned up the dust of the road.

As they galloped along furiously, one of the soldiers shouted to the others, "Do you see that wagon? Let's have a little fun with them. I'll bet we can scare them to death! When you see me do it, draw your sabers and wave them wildly as we ride."

By then everyone was watching the approaching quartet with utter terror. When the riders were two wagon lengths behind them, suddenly the cavalrymen drew their glistening sabers, waving them in the air and shouting war cries. The children screamed and everyone cowered, closing their eyes and covering their heads in any way they could, expecting fatal blows momentarily. The pounding of the hooves matched the pounding of their hearts.

Just as the soldiers drew next to them there came another huge roar of thunder. Then, in a moment, it was all over. The soldiers rode past them, continuing down the road, and as everyone looked up, they saw the soldiers halting their steeds to replace their sabers in their scabbards and then calmly continue down the road at a slow trot.

Perchik, the wagon driver, was overcome with rage as he gazed at his traumatized passengers. He had dealt with unruly soldiers before and had no fear of them. He stood up, shaking his fist at them, shouting, "You are cowards and scoundrels. How brave you are to frighten children. You are a disgrace to your country!"

Chaim turned to Perchik and exclaimed, "Perchik, my friend, what's the use. They are gone and they would never listen to us anyway. This is not a place for a human being to live anymore. I am glad we are leaving this land and I hope you will be able to do the same. Now, what can we do to protect ourselves from the storm?"

Perchik calmed himself and directed the wagon off to the side of the road. Then he shouted to everyone, "I have a canvas that I use to cover the goods I carry in the back of the wagon. Quickly, unroll it and pull one end towards me. Natan, jump down to the road, and you and I will tie it down. Everyone get under the cover as soon as you can."

The operation was completed just as the fury of the storm struck. The torrents of rain pounded down on the canvas as nature provided a dramatic show of fireworks and crashing thunder. The cover did a splendid job of protecting everyone. After half an hour the rain ended and the sun broke through the clouds. As they removed the cover they were greeted with the deeply rich and pure hues of a rainbow, nature's great gift to the human soul.

Chaim told Perchik to turn to the north on the next road. They would head to Sokolow, where he had friends who would put them up for the night.

The rest of the trip to Warsaw the following day was uneventful. They entered the huge Warsaw Ghetto, the community of thousands of Jews, where they had relatives. Before World War II there were 375,000 Jews living in Warsaw, as many as in all of France and more than in the whole country of Czechoslovakia. Only the city of New York had a larger Jewish population than Warsaw. They felt safe and secure as they planned the next phase of their odyssey.

The next day Lieutenant Korzinsky returned to the army camp. Late in the day, he was looking through the papers on his desk when he came across the notation about the four-day pass Lieutenant Kovach had issued to Natan

Zynger. Korzinsky pounded his fist on his desk and exclaimed to his adjutant, "That blockhead, didn't he realize that Zynger will most likely try to leave the country? I am going to write a note. You will take it to the telegraph office in Losice. Tell them to mark it urgent!"

Chapter 56

Passports and Visas

The Zyngers arrived in Warsaw in the late afternoon and went to the home of Dina's cousin, where they were greeted warmly. The very tired family was divided up among three relatives and put up for the night. But that same night, Chaim and Dina's cousin Aaron took Natan to the train station. Natan had secured his passport during those tense weeks when Chaim was considering whether or not to move the family to America. And, of course, Natan had his forged visa and the hope that the forgery would not be detected. The visa, which would get him into Germany and out of Poland, was now Natan's main concern.

Early that morning a telegram was read by an officer at the Warsaw army post. Captain Kotowicz sneered as he read the message, saying to his adjutant, "That Damned Korzinski, every time he loses some Jew soldier he expects me to do his dirty work. Send him this reply, 'Received your message. Am heavily committed to other duties. Will look into it next week, if possible.' Sign it for me and send it off."

It was another overcast day. A light rain was falling. As Natan stood shivering in line, waiting for his documents to be inspected, he thought about everything that had happened to him over the past few weeks: about the shock of being forced into the army, about his treatment by Wojkowski, about his mother coming to rescue him, about how he had to dig that grave, aided by poor Mendel, and how he was found by the side of the road by his father and cousin.

And now he was wondering what would come next in his life, a life that had been relatively quiet and uneventful up until this all began. Would his papers be accepted? What would it be like to take the train all the way to a strange city called Antwerp in a strange country called Belgium? Would he be able to travel all the way to America and join his brothers at last?

Suddenly he was wakened from his daydreaming with the emphatic words, "Next, papers please."

Natan, though he could not recall ever before feeling this nervous, willed himself to stay in control of his emotions as he reached for his passport and visa. The inspector opened the passport, looked at it briefly, and stamped it. Then he examined the visa. He looked at it curiously for a few moments, then, looking up at Natan, he asked, "You are taking the train through Germany and on to Belgium?"

Natan held his breath for a moment and replied, "Yes sir, that is correct."

The inspector stamped the visa and, looking past Natan, announced, "Next, papers please."

Natan boarded the train and, according to the family legend, made the trip to America in "record time."

The next day Dina's relatives came down to the train station very early with the Zynger family to see them off. Everything was going smoothly until the inspector looked at Dina's papers. After a long period of time during which the inspector picked up her visa and took it to another official, he returned and declared, "There is a problem with your visa. Another one with the same number on it has already been used, according to our records."

Dina, unfazed by the situation, responded with chutzpah, "Then one of your employees made a mistake. This is an official visa and I expect you to honor it."

"Mrs. Zynger, there may be a delay for a few days until we can verify that the visa is valid."

"That is not acceptable. We have connections with a ship to make and must leave today."

Understanding the way of their world, Dina correctly assumed that if she could find a suitably private way to offer money to the inspector and his superior, her visa would magically become valid. Dina asked the inspector if she could see his superior. He led her into the office.

After about ten minutes of nervous waiting by the family, she and the inspector returned. Dina had a smile on her face and so did the inspector, who said to her, "Have a good journey."

Chapter 57

Arrival in America

From this point forward, my story is devoid of fictional enhancement and either follows the narrative as written by Dr. Phillip Lerner in his booklet "Cousins: The Next Generation," or contains information from my cousins and their children and from my own memories and impressions.

While the train trip to Antwerp by way of Germany was relatively uneventful, it must have been extremely exciting for the four daughters, who had never been but a few kilometers outside of Losice. They probably spent hours staring out of the windows, excitedly commenting to each other about what they were seeing.

When the family reached London, they visited with their cousins, who treated them generously, outfitting the four daughters with beautiful new white dresses and shoes for an upcoming wedding and a bar mitzvah. In addition to the money Izzy and Harry had sent their father, they had insisted that the family must travel on a ship called the *Imperator*. It was one of the two or three largest passenger ships in the world at the time and one of the newest, fastest, and safest.

The family stayed in London so long that the visas they carried had expired. The authorities twice tried to dispatch the family on another ship. Chaim and Dina, on those occasions, conveniently disappeared and couldn't be located. Finally, under police escort from London (from which they were actually ready to depart anyway!), they boarded the *Imperator*, departing from Liverpool January 8, 1921, and crossing the Atlantic in eight days, during which Dina, Minicha, and Sura Basha were all frightfully seasick.

Israel and Harry traveled by train to New York, and by ferry to Ellis Island, to greet their family. (There is no record of why Natan was not with them.) They had brought along Izzy and Dorothy's second daughter, five-year-old Katie. She would be the first grandchild Chaim and Dina would see. There would be sixteen more in the years to come!

The brothers had instructed their father to buy second-class tickets, so they could disembark along with the first-class passengers immediately upon their arrival. The Ellis Island immigration officers could only work with a limited number of passengers each day. The first- and second-class passengers were processed first. Third-class and steerage passengers had to wait their turn, often having to stay on board the ship for another night.

To the dismay of the Singer brothers, the family did not disembark with the first- and second-class passengers as anticipated. Very concerned about what had happened, Israel and Harry hired a small boat and were rowed out to the ship. The family was summoned on the loudspeaker in Yiddish to come to the railing and greet the worried brothers.

Fahr Vuss? Fahr Vuss? (Why?), they shouted. The family gathered at the railing of the ship, excited to see Izzy and Harry looking so tiny far below. But since they could barely hear one another, all the brothers could understand was that everyone was fine and happy to be there. (That practice, the visits in small boats of waiting relatives to the anchored ships offshore, is preserved for posterity in photos mounted in the restored Ellis Island Museum.)

Chaim had wanted to save some money, so he had purchased third-class tickets, feeling they would need the extra money he saved in this strange new land. He managed to hold on to about $200 of the original $1200, an important windfall that came in handy that first cold winter.

They reached Cleveland on January 21, 1921.

Jennie, Dina, Pearl, Minnie, Chaim, Shirley, cousin

In America, names changed: Zynger to Singer, Shayna Chaya to Jennie, Sura Basha to Shirley, Perl to Pearl, Minicha to Mildred (or more commonly called Minnie), Natan became Nathan. Chaim became Hyman, although in his case, that name was seldom used. And as far as we know Dina was still Dina.

Initially, they all moved in with Izzy's family in their new larger home, a side by side on Westchester Avenue. Dora's brother Morris Greenbaum was part of the group as well, which at one time housed thirteen relatives.

To make their father and mother feel more welcome, the brother's first gift to the family was a complete new set of silverware, dishes, and utensils. Chaim's family lived with Izzy's family for about a year.

After moving a few times, they settled in the home that this writer well remembers, on Somerset Avenue, where Passover Seders involving all the parents, aunts and uncles, children, and grandchildren were never to-be-forgotten events. Weeks in advance, the anticipation and excitement of going to *Zaydie's* (grandfather's) house for the Passover Seder grew every day. Jewish people would greet each other with *Gut Yomtov!* (Happy Holidays!) weeks before Passover.

We would be treated to a great dinner of gefilte fish with super-potent horseradish (if you put too much on your fork it was sure to clear your sinuses!), *charoset*[10], matzo ball chicken soup, chopped liver, roasted chicken, potatoes, *kishka*[11], a compote of prunes, apricots, and pears, Passover candy jells, and lots of tasteless matzo.

Zaydie's home was on the second floor of a two-family house just like ours. I don't know where he got all the chairs and tables, but the living room and dining rooms were made into one big banquet hall, with cloth-covered tables. At one end sat Zaydie, dressed all in white, reclining on a pillow-covered chair and presiding over the service. We were given the booklet called the *Hagadah,* its contents derived from the book of Exodus. Our wine and food-stained booklets, used for many years, were printed compliments of Maxwell House Coffee.

There were many memorable events:

The hiding of the *Afikomen.* A piece of matzo is broken in half; one half is hidden, the children are asked to look for it late in the service, and the child who found it is rewarded with candy or money.

The cup for Elijah and opening the door for him. A cup is filled with wine for the prophet Elijah at every Seder. He is welcomed into the home. A tradition at our Seder was to turn off all the lights. When we were in total darkness, whoever was closest to it would open the front door. It would

---

[10] Charoset is meant to recall the mortar used by the Jews when they were slaves in Egypt; it's usually a paste-like substance made with chopped apples, nuts, cinnamon, and sweet wine.

[11] Kishka is made with a cow's intestine, stuffed and baked with various vegetables.

remain open while even in the darkness we tried to stare at Elijah's cup and imagined he had entered and was magically drinking the wine out of the glass reserved for him. (One year when the door was opened we heard the sound of footsteps in the hallway. Our imaginations ran wild! Then the lights came on, revealing one of my uncles who was late arriving and seemed to enjoy that he had scared the hell out of everyone!)

The asking of the four questions. The questions were to be asked by the youngest children. The four questions reference the "unusual practices" that take place during the Seder and are all related to the transition that carried the Hebrew people from slavery to freedom. Zaydie Singer would look over at the children and ask in Yiddish who was going to ask the *Fier Kashes* (Four Questions).

These are the questions (summarized) in order; they begin with, in Hebrew, *Ma Nishtanu Halaila Hazeh.* (Why is this night different from all other nights?)

1. Why on all other nights do we not dip vegetables in saltwater even once, while on this night we dip twice?

2. On all other nights we eat chametz (bread) or matzo. Why on this night do we eat only matzo?

3. On all other nights we eat any kind of vegetables. Why on this night do we eat only maror (bitter herbs)?

4. On all other nights we eat sitting upright or reclining. Why on this night do we all only recline?

The response to the questions were delivered by Zadie Singer and his stepson-in-law, Avrum Zalla. The following summarizes the answers:

Slavery. The saltwater into which we dip *karpas* (potato, onion, or other vegetables) represents the tears we cried while in Egypt. The charoset into which the bitter herbs are dipped reminds us of the cement we used to join the bricks in Egypt. Dipping food is considered a luxury, a sign of freedom— as opposed to the poor and enslaved, who eat "dry" and undipped foods.

Slavery. Matzo was the bread of slaves and the poor. It was cheap to produce and easy to make. Matzo also commemorates the fact that the bread did not have enough time to rise when the Jews left Egypt in haste.

Slavery. The *maror* (horseradish) reminds us of the bitterness of slavery.

Freedom. We commemorate our freedom by reclining on cushions like royalty.

Chapter 58

Life and Death in Cleveland

Chaim, listed in his passport as *melamed* (teacher), was immediately embraced by the Orthodox community in Cleveland and achieved no small measure of success and recognition in his profession. Dina, an assertive and busy businesswoman in Poland, did not adjust well in America and died at age fifty-three, a mere five and a half years after coming to America. Presumably her sudden death was from complications of dangerously high blood pressure.

After Dina died, Chaim remarried, a year to the day later, which was the custom in the Orthodox Jewish community. He married a widow, Miriam Zalla. Oddly, for many years, none of us knew her name. Our mothers all referred to her as "she," so we had the impression that the four daughters were unimpressed with their stepmother. All the stories about Dina pointed to her being an extraordinary woman whose shoes would be impossible to fill by any woman, especially in the estimation of her four adoring daughters.

Chaim Singer's reputation as scribe, calligrapher Torahs, Mezuzahs, and other religious articles in the Orthodox Jewish community continued to impact the lives of his grandchildren from time to time for many years. Cousin Irving Friedman recounted receiving an instant infusion of trust and confidence from a prospective client when his heritage was revealed. Another cousin, Allan Lerner, revealed that he gained an eternal cachet with Rabbi Engleberg of Taylor Road Synagogue when his lineage was explored during a patient encounter at Mount Sinai Hospital. Chaim Singer's extraordinary Hebrew calligraphy was preserved for generations to come when members of the family obtained and reproduced some of his framed manuscripts.

Pearl Singer Lerner shared this story that demonstrates what a unique person her father Chaim Singer was. When his family arrived in America, the Singer daughters had become old enough to get jobs of various kinds. Chaim insisted that most of the money they earned be turned over to him. Then, when one by one the daughters married, he returned all their money to them. It was perhaps in his mind a preservation of the dowry tradition practiced in Poland. Knowing he would not have enough money to provide generous dowries for four daughters, he found a creative way to solve the problem.

After Chaim Singer and his children left Izzy's home, it continued to be the first stop for all the relatives and friends Izzy encouraged to leave Poland and come to America. Izzy's devotion to his family was recounted in the reminiscences of his second daughter, Katy. She said, "He was so kind and generous to his children that if we asked him for a nickel he would give us a dime, and if we asked for a dime he would give us a quarter. When he would go on a trip he gave each of us a dollar as 'good luck money.' That then became a family tradition that was carried on by my uncle Harry, and my husband, Jerry, and I did the same with my sons."

According to his son Manuel, Izzy made frequent trips to Europe, returning each time with a relative or two. Manuel's mother Dora also told him that during that period there were never less than fourteen people and usually more at her table each night. Izzy's devotion to his family was also recalled by his sister Pearl. She said he regularly visited his parents on his way home from work every night. She suggests that on those visits Dina always had a "nosh" for him, which contributed to his becoming stout.

Izzy was always "doing for family." He bought them their first phonograph, along with a comedy record and another with the voice of a great cantor, presumably Yossele Rosenblatt. Just before Pearl's marriage to Meyer Lerner, Izzy came to visit. When he discovered only modest preparations for a simple sweet table at the wedding reception, he promptly arranged for an elaborate delicatessen-catered meal and even provided a policeman at the doorway to discourage gate-crashers. He wanted nothing to disturb his sister's wedding.

Early in 1930 Izzy explored the possibility of opening another fur business in Detroit. Apparently, that didn't work out. On his trip back to Cleveland on April 2, 1930, to rejoin his brother Harry in business, Izzy Singer, age forty-two, suddenly died of a heart attack. That left Dora a widow at age thirty-six, with four children ages five to eighteen. None of those four children are still living.

There was more tragedy to follow, when a few years later the youngest of the Singer sons, Nathan, who married his first cousin Libby Gordon (the daughter of Oscar Oxengoren, who was Dina's brother), died of a heart attack in January 1935 at age thirty-seven. Nathan and Libby had three children, Shirley, Jeanette, and Donald, all of whom are alive today.

I remember the terrible night when Nathan died. It was the night of the monthly "I. Singer Unity Club" meeting. I was seven years old and sleeping with my cousins at the home of my Aunt Jennie and Uncle Norman. They came home from the meeting and tearfully broke the news of our uncle's death.

The curse of tragedies in the Singer family claimed yet another victim: Norman Friedman, the husband of Jennie Singer Friedman, was a cancer victim and died on Mother's Day in 1947, at age forty-four. I vividly recall visiting Uncle Norman a few days before his death, and for the first time in my life seeing someone with the haunted yellow of a fatally jaundiced person. Aunt Jenny was another widow with three children, Donald, Rosalind, and Irving, all of whom are deceased.

Manuel Singer recounted how when his father died in 1930, in the midst of the Great Depression, the bank paid his mother only ten cents on the dollar for his money, leaving her in poverty with three children to raise. Since Dora had married so young she had no particular saleable skills, so Harry Singer gave her money to enroll in beautician school. She earned her license and opened her own beauty shop in the back of Rabinowitz's Barber Shop, on Kinsman Avenue near 153rd, and eked out a meager living.

Manuel, Debra and Harry sharing a cocktail

With the death of his brother Izzy, his Uncle Harry became a father figure to Manuel Singer and the other members of his family. Manuel recalled how when he was about to leave for overseas duty in World War II, Harry flew to Savanah, Georgia, to "share a cocktail and see him off." Harry also walked him down the aisle at his wedding in Louisville, Kentucky, when he married Debra June Hoffman in 1950.

This recollection about Harry Singer is from his son Edwin Z. Singer: "My father had a strong sense of responsibility toward his siblings and their offspring, particularly for the families of his brothers, both of whom died very young. His career in the fur business provided many in the family with both full- and part-time employment. He was very supportive of the I. Singer Unity Club and the Family Free Loan Society, both devoted to accommodating the social and capital needs of new arrivals, family and *landsleit* (other Jews from the home land), to this country. He was active in the community (Masonic Lodge, Mezricher Society, Board of Trustees of the Orthodox Jewish Children's Home…) and was a generous contributor to synagogues and the Jewish Welfare Fund. At the fur shop a cigar box with dollar bills was available to the secretaries, for distributing to the itinerant solicitors for Jewish congregations."

I recall my Uncle Harry as a quiet, thoughtful, and serious man who had the respect of everyone in the family. I always suspected he did more for family members than most of us knew about. I was certain he gave money to our grandfather Chaim. But I also suspect that during the Depression when we were very poor, either Chaim then gave some of that money to my mother or Harry helped us out from time to time.

A favorite story about Harry is how when he and his wife—my Aunt Frieda, who was also Harry's bookkeeper—were on a trip to Cuba after World War II, Frieda had passport and birth certificate problems during re-entry into the USA, and Harry was quoted as saying to the authorities, "You may keep my wife, but not my bookkeeper."

Max Levine, Norman Friedman, unknown, Alvin Friedman, unknown, Harry Singer, Jennie Caputo, Meyer Lerner at the fur shop

Chapter 59

The I. Singer Unity Club

Sometime in the early 1930s, during the depths of the Depression years, the Singers formed a family club. As children we knew the name as merely the "Family Club," but later we learned its official name was the I. Singer Unity Club (named for Izzy).

Many such clubs existed. Like ours, they were formed by immigrant families as mutual benefit societies. The "Family Club" would meet once a month at member's homes, conduct a business meeting, collect dues, enjoy food prepared by the hosts, and afterward play cards. The dues they collected would be deposited in a bank and made available to members of the family, to help them out for a variety of reasons. I wasn't aware of who was being helped and why until, in 1954 when I needed money to build a home, my mother obtained a $1,000 gift from the club for me and my wife, Sally.

In addition to the monthly meetings, they held an annual family picnic in a park located in a Cleveland suburb along Lake Erie. The food and drink were mainly things like kosher hamburgers and hot dogs, potato salad, pie, soda pop, and a keg of beer. There were races and a softball game, in which everyone wanted to be on Uncle Dave Saltzman's team. He was the youngest, tallest, and most athletic of all the uncles and the only one of our uncles who was American-born. Dave Saltzman hit a home run every time he batted.

There were originally eighteen first cousins in the Singer family, the children of the three brothers and the four sisters. Except for the four children of Izzy Singer, who lived in Lexington, Kentucky, all the rest who lived in Cleveland were very close. Whoever married into the family in my mother's generation was instantly accepted as a full-fledged member.

There was one particularly interesting relationship in the family. Harry Singer married Frieda Friedman, who was born in Sokolow, Poland, a town near Losice. Then Harry's sister Jennie married Frieda's brother Norman. My cousins, their children, considered themselves "double cousins." Additionally, I recall that we thought of the siblings of Frieda and Norman, their brothers Morton and Alvin, and their wives as our uncles and aunts, which, of course, they were not.

The closeness of the family was remarkable, especially in the early years.

The reasons are easy to understand. Initially, most everyone lived in the same neighborhood, mainly in homes off of East 105th Street between Superior Avenue and St. Clair Avenue. We went to the same schools, attended the same synagogues, and shopped in the same stores. Several of the men worked in the fur shop known as André Schwartz Singer. Uncle Harry was the Singer.

Everyone attended family life cycle events like bar mitzvahs, weddings, and funerals. I, and many of my cousins, worked in family businesses. I worked summers at the fur shop, and at Uncle Dave's grocery store as well as my father's tobacco shop. Gradually some families left East 105th street for other areas of Cleveland, for Cleveland Heights or the Jewish neighborhood off Kinsman Avenue. But we still managed to remain close.

While a lot of Yiddish was spoken by our parents, it is interesting to note that they almost never spoke Polish or Russian, the languages of their native countries. They were always striving to become as Americanized as they could. My parents, and the parents of my cousins, wanted us to live the "American Dream." They encouraged us to work hard and get good grades in school, so we could live a better life than they had known. As we look at the next generation of cousins, we will understand the rationale for this book's original working title, "From the Shoemaker to the Philanthropists."

Chaim Singer's children's generation of the I. Singer Unity Club

Chaim Singer's Grandchildren's generation

The Cousins in recent years. Bill is front right.

Epilogue
The Philanthropists

In using the word "philanthropists" for the purposes of my story, I am utilizing dictionary definitions such as "implies interest in the general human welfare," or "a desire to help mankind." Using that broad a definition, I have not limited my account to those who had the means and made substantial charitable gifts (though there were many of those included here!) but have also included those who worked at professions serving the general public and the nation, in various fields including the military, medicine, engineering, education, and the arts.

Had Avrum Binstock not established a shoe-making factory in his home in Losice and employed his nephew Israel Singer, and then helped Israel and later Harry Singer come to America, and had Israel and Harry Singer not been able to bring the rest of the Singer family to America, their father and mother, brother, four sisters—and whoever they married, along with their children—would all have perished in the Holocaust. Instead, the children of Chaim and Dina Singer, all safely in America, all married and had a total of eighteen children, nine girls and nine boys.

Still living today are five men and four women. The oldest of the females were still of a generation where the expectation was to marry young and dedicate their lives to taking care of their husbands, their children, and their homes. However, I do not want to in any way devalue the contributions made to society by my nine female cousins. They all were wonderful women, and the surviving cousins, Shirley Silver, Jeanette Berman, Deanie Wainstein, and Helene Krasney are no exception. Most of them grew up during the Great Depression and faced difficult times, which made them stronger human beings and good mothers to their children. Of the nine women, four or possibly five had some college education. Shirley Singer Felber, daughter of Harry and Frieda Singer, earned a bachelor's degree at Ohio State and taught school briefly before marrying Joe Felber. The two youngest of the cousins, Deanie and Helene (daughters of Minnie Singer and Dave Saltzman), earned college degrees: Deanie, a bachelor's in Education from Ohio State University and Helene a degree from the Pratt Institute. Deanie, wife of Dr. Mayer Wainstein, taught in Ohio briefly. These days she serves as a volunteer at the

Toledo Art Museum. Helene Saltzman Krasney is a professional graphic artist.

The only one of the women who was in a position to make substantial philanthropic contributions was the late Rosalind (Roz) Friedman (who died at age eighty-four in 2015), the widow of Sam Krasney and the mother of four daughters, Nora, Paula, Sherry, and Donna. In the 1930s and '40s the Friedmans lived in a two-story house on East 153rd Street in Cleveland. The Krasneys, with their three sons, lived on the second floor. Their youngest son, Samuel, was in love with Roz, who at first was not interested in "the boy upstairs." Eventually she recognized his qualities, quit her studies at Ohio State, and married Sam, a brilliant man who was one of the youngest to ever earn a CPA in the state of Ohio. He founded a very successful accounting firm. Using his knowledge of tax law and his business acumen, he began to buy companies, starting with Banner Trucking. Banner Trucking became Banner Industries, an international industrial conglomerate that included dozens of businesses in the US, Europe, Hong Kong, and Japan. Together Sam and Roz made many charitable contributions, and after his death she continued giving charitably to a variety of institutions and causes. In addition to direct donations, Sam and Roz donated whole buildings, including a recreation center for the Israel Defense Forces in Northern Israel, a dormitory for the Telshe Yeshiva Orthodox Jewish School in Israel, and a library for the Hebrew Academy of Cleveland. Other major contributions included Friends of the Israel Defense Forces, Menorah Park, Cleveland Jewish Community Federation, and University Hospital. There were numerous other donations for education, medical research, and the homeless. The Krasney daughters recall that nearly every Sunday, rabbis and religious students would come to their door and ask for donations. Roz always gave.

Manuel "Kelly" Singer, 1925-2010 the youngest child and only son of Israel and Dora Singer, was born in Lexington, Kentucky. While in high school he was a member of his high school's Kentucky State Championship golf team. He proudly played the clarinet in the school orchestra and a local dance band. At age seventeen he enlisted in the Air Force during World War II, and saw action as a B-17 bomber navigator in combat missions in Europe. After graduation from the University of Kentucky he married Debra Hoffman. They had two children, David Lee Singer and Patti Singer. Manuel spent several years touring the United States and Central and South America as one of the founders of the frozen drink company ICEE. When they returned to Kentucky, he and Debra formed Signcrafters, the first computer based sign company in Louisville. Over the next twenty years they were recognized with many awards including The Better Business Bureau award for ethics in business, the Board of Education Award for mentoring middle school children, The Gold Award from the Chamber of Commerce and the Sam Walton Business Leader Award. "Kelly was often complimented on having the same staff at Signcrafters for so many years. His philosophy? "You can't quit and I can't fire you!"

As to Manuel's three sisters, Lillian, Kay, and Shirley, the only specific information about their philanthropy I have found is that Lillian was elected chairperson of the Lexington branch of The National Council of Jewish Women.

Unlike his cousin Manuel, Donald Singer, born in 1927, son of Nathan, lived in Cleveland his entire life. As a result of the shock of the sudden death of his father when Donald was seven, he was afflicted with a terrible stutter, which stayed with him for most of his life. But he didn't let that handicap deter him. He—along with his mother, Libby, and sisters Shirley and Jeanette—were perhaps the poorest family of any of the Singer cousins. They lived in a two-bedroom, one-bathroom home, where Donald had to sleep on the sofa. But they survived nicely because they lived in a two-story home filled with close, supportive grandparents, uncles, and aunts. Donald worked summers at the White Motor Company. Both Shirley and Jeanette also worked there during World War II. Somehow Donald was able to make enough money to attend Ohio State University and earn a Bachelor of Business Administration. After graduation he got a job as an office manager in a scrap metal business, working there for ten years. He related how one day he was in the office when the police came in, arrested, and handcuffed his boss, the owner of the business, for fraudulently adding weight to his truckloads of scrap. Donald quit the business that very day. Because he knew how much money could be made in the business without cheating, he set about establishing his own business. He founded Miles Alloy on Cleveland's south side. Over the years, as his business grew, he trained his three nephews, Neal, Bruce, and Ozzie Berman—the sons of his sister Jeanette and her husband Irv Berman—in how to operate a scrap business. They subsequently moved to Atlanta, Georgia, where they established their own very successful scrap business.

Donald Friedman, (1926-1993), son of Norman Friedman and Jennie Singer Friedman, was born in Cleveland. He had either a photographic memory or an enormous aptitude for learning, or most likely both. Always an outstanding student, he also played piano and clarinet. After high school graduation in 1944 he enlisted in the ASTP (Army Specialized Training Program) and was sent to Ohio State University to study engineering. When the war ended he was sent back to the regular army to play clarinet in an army band. After his army stint he re-enrolled at Ohio State, to get his degree as a civil engineer. While working for the State Highway Department he obtained a law degree from the Cleveland Marshall Law School. He never actually practiced law. Instead, he joined his brother-in-law's firm when he obtained his license as a Certified Public Accountant. Donald and his wife, Ruth, had three daughters, Cindy and twins Nora and Laura. A third-degree Mason,

Donald was active in the Kidney Foundation, was a member of the Cleveland Jewish Federation, and donated to the Salvation Army, the Red Cross, and the Holocaust Memorial. He was a staunch supporter of Israel.

Irving Z. Friedman (1932–2007) was the younger brother of Donald and Roz Friedman. After he graduated from Western Reserve University he went into the Air Force, stationed in Korea and Wilmington, Ohio, with the rank of captain. When he returned and obtained his CPA he joined with his brother-in-law Sam Krasney and formed the accounting firm Krasney, Polk, and Friedman. Irving and his wife, Charlotte, had two daughters, Norma and Ellen, and two sons, Paul and Steve. In addition to his work as an accountant, he owned and managed real estate in Ohio, Pennsylvania, and Florida and was involved in several businesses over the years, including a company called Stainsafe that did business in the US, Canada, and parts of Europe. His philanthropy involved the Cleveland Jewish Federation, Hebrew Academy, Gross Shechter Day School, Chabad, Israel Bonds, and the Meyer Academy in Florida. His most important philanthropic motivation was to help to continue the legacy of the Jewish people.

Bill Nemoyten, who was born in 1928, son of Shirley Singer Nemoyten and Jacob Nemoyten, took a different path—in fact, several different paths. A talented musician who at eighteen joined the musician's union right out of high school, he set his sights on becoming a music teacher. After graduating from Western Reserve University with a bachelor of science degree, he later acquired a master's degree at Kent State University. Bill taught instrumental and vocal music in Ohio for seventeen years, building an outstanding band program. In 1967 Bill wrote and then administered a federal grant program that employed musicians for ninety-nine performances in the Summit County Schools. Bill was then offered a position as the first full-time paid manager of the Greater Akron Musical Association, which operated the Akron Symphony, Symphony Chorus, and Youth Symphony.

In 1969, Bill took his wife, Sally, and their four children, Jo, Mark, David, and Susan to Quincy, Illinois, where he had been engaged as Executive Director of the Quincy Society of Arts, America's oldest community arts council. In 1972 Bill accepted a job as executive director of the San Mateo County, California Arts Council. Following the passing of California's Property 13 in 1978, removing nearly all administrative funding, Bill changed careers once again and became the administrator of Peninsula Temple Beth El in San Mateo, a six-hundred-family-member reform synagogue. Bill and Sally were particularly proud to receive the David Ben-Gurion Award from State of Israel Bonds in 1984. After becoming involved in the establishment of the first Jewish cemetery on the San Francisco Peninsula, Bill resigned from the Temple to become a licensed cemetery broker. Bill's wife of thirty-four years, Sally, died a victim of breast cancer in 1985. He married Barbara Levy two years later. Bill returned to his first love as an instrumental music teacher in San Leandro, California, until his retirement in 1993.

Other items of note about Bill Nemoyten include that he was elected chairman of a national confederation of community arts councils; earned a certificate in arts administration from Harvard University; wrote a piece of music that was performed for the hundredth anniversary of Temple Israel of Akron. He conducted his concert band composition, "The Cuyahoga Valley Suite," at the Blossom Music Center with the Woodridge High School Band, and for performances by the Golden Gate Park Band in San Francisco. Bill also taught Arts Administration at University of California Extension, performed his "Hornman" show in California, Nevada, Arizona, and Florida, and wrote and published his memoir, "It All Started With a Trombone."

Edwin Z. Singer, born in Cleveland in 1930, son of Harry Singer and Frieda Friedman Singer, graduated from Ohio State with a degree in accounting. He also earned a law degree at Case Western Reserve Law School in 1953 and married Naomi Greenfield that same year. After practicing accounting while still in law school, he went into business in Sandusky, Ohio, with his brother-in-law, Joe Felber, and another partner, David Wiggins. They operated a chain of twenty-three discount department stores called Mr. Wiggs. He later went into business in Lexington, Kentucky, with Arthur (Babe) Myers, husband of Shirley Singer, who was the daughter of Israel Singer. After having sold their interest in the Mr. Wiggs business, Ed and Joe returned to Cleveland from Sandusky and established a new business: Arrow Distributing, a "rack jobber" of CDs in the pre-recorded music area. The company is now owned and operated by the children (Harry, Phillip, and Diane) and the grandchildren of Ed and Naomi Singer. Arrow distributes to college bookstores throughout the country and is also an owner and operator of commercial real estate.

While living in Sandusky, Ed became president of Oheb Shalom Temple and was on the board of Providence Hospital. After returning to Cleveland, Ed's involvement in Jewish organizations has become legendary: he is president of Menorah Park, one of the largest senior care facilities (355 beds) in the United States; and the Menorah Park Foundation. He served as treasurer of Brith Emeth Congregation, on the board of Fairhill Center and Beachbrook, and served as president of the Commission of Cemetery Preservation. He is proudest of the award he received from the Association of Fundraising Professionals, as the outstanding volunteer of the year 2012. His comment about that award is, "The Talmud says, greater than one who does a mitzvah is one who causes others to do a mitzvah." Ed is also especially proud of his wife, Naomi, who served on the board of trustees of the world-famous Cleveland Orchestra.

Burt Saltzman, born in 1937, son of Mildred (Minnie) Singer Saltzman and Dave Saltzman, grew up working in his dad's grocery store at 33rd and Payne Avenue in Cleveland. The business had started out as a fruit and vegetable stand started by Burt's grandfather Alex in 1920. When his father, Dave, took it over he made it into a full-service market. Burt went to Ohio State University, where he was in the ROTC and earned a degree in business administration. After graduation he joined the US Army, Quartermaster Corps. When he returned he suggested to his dad that they open a second store, but Dave felt they had their hands full with the one store. But the knowledge about business Burt had gained in college led him to indeed open that second market and then a third one. The years passed. Dave Saltzman died. Burt married Judy Zwick in 1959. They had twin daughters, Trudy and Stacy, and when Burt brought their two sons, Dan and Steven, into the business they continued to add more stores to the chain. Dave's Market now numbers fourteen stores, most of which are full-service and a couple of which are smaller "boutique" markets.

Burt Saltzman has been honored by the Cleveland community for his willingness to open and operate full-service supermarkets in poorer areas shunned by other grocery chains. His generosity to area churches and synagogues and to the poor is legendary in Cleveland. His office wall is covered with plaques and testimonials lauding his generosity. Many articles about his dedication to his employees and his community can be found in the archives of the *Cleveland Plain Dealer* newspaper. He has been recognized for his support of neighborhood hunger centers, the Cleveland Food Bank, Salvation Army, at least fifteen churches, Cleveland Jewish Federation, Menorah Park Foundation, and many others. Burt is well known for his "over the top" work habits. Now in his eighties, he still goes to work every day and vacations only briefly once or twice a year.

The "Doctors Lerner" made it possible for Pearl Singer Lerner, the wife of Meyer Lerner, to declare what most women of her generation would adore saying, "my son, the doctor"—twice. According to her son, Dr. Allan Lerner, because her two sons were doctors, their mother somehow felt qualified to offer her free diagnoses of illnesses that were visited upon relatives.

Phillip Lerner (1933-2012), the older of the two Lerner doctors, earned his medical degree at Western Reserve University Medical School, under the tutelage of some outstanding teachers including the famous Dr. Benjamin Spock, author of the bestselling book, "Baby and Child Care." Following his residency at Boston's Beth Israel Hospital, Phillip became affiliated with a nationally respected medical researcher at the Tufts University Medical School. Listed along with his mentor, Dr. Louis Weinstein, in a four-part series in the prestigious *New England Journal of Medicine*, Dr. Lerner had a career that was greatly accelerated when he became recognized for his research work on a medical condition called infective endocarditis. While in Boston, Phillip met and fell in love with Ronnie Hober. They eloped in in 1958, causing quite a stir in family circles. Aunt Shirley expected the worst when she first met Ronnie, who was wearing a stylish but suspicious Empire-style dress, popular at the time. Their son, Dr. Barron Lerner, was born in 1960, and their daughter, Dr. Dana Lerner, in 1963.

Over the years Phillip was a frequent contributor to medical journals. He returned to Cleveland in 1966 as chief of infectious diseases at the Cleveland VA hospital and was a professor at what later became the Case Western Reserve University Medical School. In 1973 he was named chief of infectious diseases at Cleveland's Mount Sinai Hospital. Dr. Lerner had acquired an international medical reputation and was invited to speak at medical conferences, including one in China and another in Shiaz, Iran. Based on the meticulous journals he kept, Dr. Barron Lerner, Phillip Lerner's son, wrote a fascinating book entitled *The Good Doctor.*

Allan Lerner, born in 1936, also earned his medical degree at Western Reserve University, where he was also a student of Dr. Benjamin Spock. Following his time as a Navy doctor, he became an internal radiologist at Cleveland's Mount Sinai Hospital, at the time when Arteriography first began to be widely used for diagnoses. He was on the staff of Mount Sinai from 1962 to 2000. Other activities included board membership in Physicians for Social Responsibility and The Gathering Place (cancer support organization), and volunteering as an instructor in radiology at Case Western Reserve University Medical School. Allan's wife is Nancy and his two children are David and Carey. On a very special personal note, which dramatically demonstrates the close family bonds among the Singer cousins, both Doctors Lerner left their very demanding duties in Cleveland for a few days and flew to California to support me and our family at the time of my wife Sally's death.

While none of the children of Chaim Singer was able to earn a college degree, their children, the eighteen Singer cousins, earned twelve bachelor's degrees, two law degrees, one master's degree, and two doctorates in medicine. Some served in the armed forces. The doctors treated thousands of patients and saved countless numbers of lives. The businessmen and women established and/or expanded dozens of businesses, creating jobs for thousands of workers. They gave and continue to give millions of dollars to charities. They all married and, while most of them live in Ohio, one group lived in Kentucky and one in California. They had a total of forty-nine children, who live in New York, Ohio, Illinois, Texas, Georgia, Florida, Oregon, and England.

And now, as we come to the conclusion of this tale, we shall examine what truly happened (or as close as we can find to the truth) to the man who made all of this possible. Avrum Binstock and his wife, Faiga, eventually were the parents of four girls and two boys. The family story is that in 1941, Avrum and Faiga knew the Nazis were coming and fled to a nearby town. They were captured and all but the two sons, Herschel and Beryl, were murdered by the

Faiga and Avrum seated in the middle

Nazis. Herschel was an Auschwitz survivor. Beryl must have been captured by the Russians. He was sent to Siberia with his wife and daughter. After the war they were able to move to Israel. The daughter still lives there and has two married sons. Another member of the Binstock family went to Israel. He married and had a boy and a girl. The boy, Abram Binstock, was killed in the battle for Jerusalem during the Six Day War.

Leah, Allen and Herschel Binstock

After World War II, Herschel Binstock met and married Leah Konigsberg, who was from Jarslow, Poland, and has her own amazing story of Holocaust survival. They had a son, Allen, and in 1949, with the help of a Jewish agency they were brought to Bellevue, Illinois. Incredibly, after surviving the hell of the Holocaust, they faced antisemitism in the Bellevue community. They then reached out to Harry Singer, who sponsored their move to Cleveland. Harry secured a loan from the I. Singer Family Club and helped set Herschel Binstock up in a shoe repair business. Herschel Binstock died several years ago. The three Binstock children are Allen, a lawyer for the National Labor Relations Board in Cleveland, Fred, a certified public accountant, and daughter Gloria Triester, who is a board-certified holistic health practitioner and coach. Their mother, Leah, is now ninety years old.

And so, as we end this blended tale of fiction and fact we discover that if it was indeed true that Avrum Binstock, the shoemaker, helped Israel Singer come to America, our nation and the state of Israel benefitted enormously from the philanthropy of the descendants of Chaim Singer, and descendants of Avrum Binstock will benefit as well, for generations to come.

As to the more than fifty members of the next generation of the Singer and Binstock families, they are a remarkable group of individuals who continue to enrich America. Someday hopefully someone will tell their story.

The Author

Bill Nemoyten was brought up in Cleveland, Ohio in an orthodox Jewish home. He was one of eighteen first cousins, all first-generation Americans. His love for and pride in his family is demonstrated throughout this book which is enriched by his many fond memories of a style of Jewish life when most of his uncles and aunts frequently spoke Yiddish to one another. Although, as a boy, Bill attended an orthodox Yeshiva and had a very traditional Bar Mitzvah, as an adult, he joined a reform temple in Akron, Ohio and later spent six years as the administrator of Peninsula Temple Beth El in San Mateo, California. His journey through Judaism has taken him to Kol Hadash, a secular humanist congregation, where he is an active member and sounds the Shofar each year on Rosh Hashana and Yom Kippur.

Bill's education includes a Bachelor of Science from Case Western University, a Master of Education from Kent State University and a Certificate in Arts Administration from Harvard University.

Bill began writing this book in 2011 when he was eighty-one and completed it in his eighty-ninth year! He published his memoir, "It All Started with a Trombone" (Available on Amazon) in 2012. Besides many stories of growing up in Cleveland, starting a family and other life adventures, it covers his time as a school band director, musical performer, composer, symphony orchestra manager, arts council director, temple administrator and businessman. As the creator and performer of *The Hornman Show* (now *The HornMEN Show*, which he does with his son, Mark Nemoyten, a professional trumpet player and music teacher) he has delighted and educated audiences of all ages and sizes in the San Francisco Bay Area and around the U.S.

For more information about Bill and The Hornman, please visit www.thehornman.com.